# Secret Kisses & Twilight Wishes

## THE THATCHER BROTHERS OF ACORN FIELD HEIGHTS

### BOOK THREE

## MAGGIE ELLIS

First published in the United States of America in October 2025.

Cover Design by InkVault Publishing

ISBN 978-1-953139-29-0 (Ebook)

ISBN 978-1-953139-38-2 (Paperback)

First Edition

10 9 8 7 6 5 4 3 2 1

# Also by Maggie Ellis

## STANDALONES

*The Christmas Cabin Mix-Up*

---

## THE THATCHER BROTHERS OF ACORN FIELD HEIGHTS

*Pumpkin Kisses & Harvest Wishes*
*Cinnamon Kisses & Forever Wishes*
*Secret Kisses & Twilight Wishes*

# Chapter One

## QUINN

I was overdressed, and everyone knew it. The velvet blazer that made me feel like a creative professional in the city made me look like I'd wandered off a period drama set here in Acorn Field Heights, where flannel was apparently formal wear. Twenty faces turned toward me as I stepped into the town hall basement, and I could feel them staring at every vintage button on my plum-colored jacket.

The flannel-to-velvet ratio in this room was approximately 20:1, and I was the one.

I chose a seat in the back row, setting my portfolio on my knees and trying to look like someone who belonged. The basement smelled like burnt coffee and fifty years of committee meetings, with fluorescent lights that made everyone look vaguely ill. Old wiring snaked across the ceiling—exposed cloth insulation in places, the kind that made fire marshals nervous. Metal folding chairs scraped against linoleum as people settled in.

My phone buzzed in my pocket. Fifteen percent battery, even though I'd charged it this morning. The thing was dying a slow death, but between rent and inventory costs and keeping Enchanted Threads afloat these past three months, a new phone wasn't exactly priority spending.

My gaze drifted across the room when it snagged on the guy in the corner.

He sat apart from everyone else, one ankle crossed over his knee, a worn notebook balanced on his thigh. Dark hair fell across his forehead as he bent over the page. Even from fifteen feet away I could see his pencil moving in quick strokes. He wore a dark green flannel shirt rolled to his elbows, revealing forearms marked by thin white scars—the kind that came from working with tools or climbing trees as a kid.

His hands moved across the page. Long fingers, callused at the tips. I watched one hand shift his pencil grip while the other braced the notebook. My pulse jumped for a second, watching how intently focused he was on the page. Mud stains marked his jeans along with a patched tear.

He glanced up. His gaze met mine across the room—gray-green, like sea glass. My breath caught. Then he was back to his notebook, but heat climbed up my neck.

"You must be Quinn."

I jumped. A woman with silver hair and a kind smile stood next to my chair, holding a clipboard.

"Caroline Thatcher, but everyone calls me Aunt Caroline. I run Harvest Moon Café." She handed me a paper cup of coffee that looked strong enough to wake the dead. "Welcome to town."

"Thank you." I accepted the coffee, wrapping my hands around it. "Still finding my way around."

"Three months is hardly enough time to settle in, but you're doing wonderfully." She smiled. "Your shop is lovely."

Before I could respond, a man in his sixties clapped his hands twice.

"Alright, everyone. Let's get started." Mayor Goldwin consulted his clipboard. "We are just three weeks out from the fall festival. That means we're behind schedule and need all hands on deck."

Mayor Goldwin worked through his agenda. Booth assignments, parking logistics, corn maze updates. I tried to focus, but my attention kept drifting to Corner Guy. His pencil never stopped moving.

"Quinn Fairchild opened Enchanted Threads on Main Street back in July," Mayor Goldwin said. "Quinn, would you like to tell us about your booth idea?"

Every head swiveled toward me.

I stood, smoothing my blazer with damp palms. "Hi, everyone. Thank you for letting me participate." I opened my portfolio. "I was thinking we could set up a Halloween costume photo booth. Professional backdrop, vintage props, some pieces from my shop that people could borrow for photos."

Silence. Someone coughed.

"Families love this kind of thing," I continued, talking too fast. "It creates shareable content for social media, which helps promote the festival—"

"What kind of costumes?" a woman near the front interrupted.

"Sorry?"

"What kind of costumes would people borrow? My kids are picky."

Relief flooded through me. "Everything from authentic Victorian— I have an 1880s bustle gown with original jet beading—to 1920s flapper dresses. For kids, I've got pirates with real brass buckles, a whole collection of 1950s poodle skirts. All professionally cleaned, all historically accurate."

"I love it," someone else said.

"Me too," another voice added. "The social media aspect is brilliant!" The young woman who spoke seemed to be about my age, and she sat with her phone in her hands.

"Thanks." I relaxed a bit. "I was also thinking quick costume consultations. Help people put together looks using pieces they already own, plus maybe one or two rental items. Make it accessible for families on a budget."

A sharp snap made me lose my train of thought. The artist guy's pencil tip broke against his notebook. He didn't look up, just reached into his shirt pocket for another pencil.

"Sounds perfect," Mayor Goldwin said. "We'll put you near the gazebo." He scanned the room. "You'll need help with setup. Asher, you've got an artistic eye. You'll work with Quinn on this."

The pencil went still.

Asher—so that was his name—looked up. His eyes met mine, and I registered the same gray-green from before. Something careful lived in that gaze, like he was already calculating distance.

"Sure," he said. His voice was low, rough around the edges. "I'll text you."

That was it. He was already back to his notebook before Mayor Goldwin moved on.

The meeting continued for another thirty minutes, but I'd lost the thread. My phone buzzed in my pocket—probably Carter again. He'd been calling more frequently lately, leaving messages about "reconnecting" that made my skin crawl. I'd stopped answering two months ago, but he'd never been good at respecting boundaries.

When Mayor Goldwin finally adjourned, I gathered my portfolio. Several people smiled at me as they passed. I turned to find Asher already halfway to the door.

My feet moved before my brain caught up. I squeezed through the crowd and caught him just as he pushed open the exit door.

"Hey," I called.

He stopped, one hand on the door, and turned back. Up close, I could see he was probably late twenties, with sharp cheekbones and a small scar cutting through his left eyebrow. Paint stains dotted his flannel.

"I'm Quinn. I guess we're working together?"

"Looks that way."

I waited. He didn't add anything.

The silence stretched awkwardly. I fumbled with my portfolio, and the clasp popped open. Papers exploded everywhere—sketches, fabric samples, vendor contacts scattering across the floor.

"Perfect," I muttered, dropping to my knees.

Asher crouched down at the same moment, placing his book on the ground. We nearly collided, heads missing by inches. His hand landed on top of mine as we both reached for the same sketch. For a heartbeat we froze there, too close, his gray-green eyes meeting mine with an intensity that stole my breath.

Then he pulled back, gathering papers. His gaze caught on one of my inventory lists. "You've got good organization. Organized by era?"

"Makes it easier to track rentals." My voice came out breathier than intended. "And repairs."

He handed me the stack, fingers brushing mine. "Smart."

It was the first real thing he'd said to me, and I stared like he'd just recited poetry.

"So maybe we should meet this week?" I stood, shoving papers back into my portfolio. "Go over the design—"

"I'll text you." He was already turning away.

"Right, but when?" I pulled out a business card—cream with purple script—and held it out.

He took it without really looking, shoving it into his back pocket. "I'll be in touch."

Then he was gone.

I stood there, papers still half-hanging out, watching through the door's small window as he crossed to a beat-up truck. He moved with his shoulders hunched against the wind.

"Don't mind Asher."

I turned to find Aunt Caroline beside me.

"He's a good kid. Just needs time to warm up. He's the youngest of his brothers, my nephews. He'll be perfect for you."

"Excuse me?"

"I mean, he's become the town's handyman since he returned home from college. He'll be the perfect match for you." She paused with a suspicious smirk. "And your booth."

"Of course." I forced a smile.

Aunt Caroline patted my arm and headed back inside.

I pushed open the door. The October air bit through my blazer as the village green stretched dark ahead of me. In three weeks this space would be full of booths and families.

If I was still here. If I hadn't already failed at fitting in.

My car sat two blocks down. I walked past the hardware store, past Harvest Moon Café with its cinnamon-scented air, past the closed bakery. And then I saw it.

Enchanted Threads.

My shop. My sign in gold and purple script. Through the window I could see the vintage mannequins, the costume racks, the Victorian fainting couch I'd reupholstered.

I'd built this. After Carter and his control issues and the slow erosion of my sense of self, I'd packed up my life and started over.

Three months of fourteen-hour days and mounting debt, but I'd built this.

A man who couldn't say more than five words didn't change that.

I unlocked my car and slid in, tossing my portfolio onto the passenger seat. Something tumbled off and landed in my lap—a worn notebook with a leather cover.

My breath caught.

Asher's notebook.

I must've grabbed it when he was helping me pick up my papers. It'd been an accident, of course. I knew I should leave it alone. But my fingers seemed to have a mind of their own since they were already opening the cover.

The first page held a detailed sketch of the town square, every architectural detail drawn with care. I turned the page. It was a sunrise—or sunset, I couldn't be sure—with a barn in the foreground and a horse running in a pasture. The next page showed more landscape sketches, then a portrait of an elderly woman, then Main Street storefronts.

And then I found it.

"Festival booth" written at the top in sharp handwriting. Below it, rough concept sketches—a backdrop with autumn leaves, prop placement, a floor plan. Notes in the margins: "Lighting important," "Vintage camera on tripod?" "Check about color scheme."

My throat went tight.

He'd been paying attention. Listening to my pitch and sketching ideas while I talked.

My phone buzzed. Unknown number.

> This is Asher Thatcher. Saturday 9am, your shop. I'll bring preliminary sketches.

I stared at the text a few seconds longer than necessary before responding.

> Sounds good. See you then.

I hit send, then added another message.

> PS - You left your notebook at the meeting. I
> have it if you need it before Saturday.

Three dots appeared. Disappeared. Appeared again.

> Keep it until Saturday. I'll get it back then.

I tucked the notebook into my portfolio and started my car. The drive to my rental cottage took three minutes.

Inside, I made tea and changed into sweats and wrapped up my frizzy orange hair into *the messiest of buns.*

*It* didn't take lo*ng before* I was thinking about him. About the contradiction between his distance and his sketches. About the way his pencil had moved with the same focused attention I'd seen in his eyes. About those paint stains that made me think he created things with hands that knew how to be gentle and sure.

I fell asleep with his notebook on my nightstand.

# Chapter Two

## ASHER

The shelf measurements were wrong. Not that it was Isla's fault. She was stressed as it was, and had probably tried to take them herself between customers. I stood in the back room of Sugar & Spice Bakery, holding my tape measure and staring at the wall like it might confess to moving overnight. According to Isla's sketch, the shelving unit should fit with three inches of clearance on either side. According to reality, I had maybe an inch and a half. Maybe.

"Isla?" I called toward the front. "Where'd you want these shelves? The measurements aren't—"

I stepped through the doorway and stopped dead.

Sawyer, my older middle brother, stood in the middle of the bakery, looking like a man facing a firing squad. Which, he kind of was. I hadn't expected him to be here. In fact, I was fairly certain he'd been avoiding the place like it held the plague. Just as I started wondering why he'd decided to ruin his life further, I noticed the little girl in a purple tutu next to him who was staring at Isla with a wide grin.

Oh, that made more sense. My niece had probably dragged him in. Poor Sawyer. Here. In Isla's bakery. The place he'd been avoiding for two solid months.

"Oh. Sawyer." I couldn't quite keep the surprise out of my voice. "You're... here."

"And you're here," Sawyer said at the same time my adorable niece, Maple, said, "Can I sit at that table? Please? I don't want to drop crumbs on the floor because that would be rude, and Daddy says we're always polite to princesses."

The tension in the room was thick enough to slice with one of Isla's bread knives. I'd been there when Sawyer had left. I knew their history. The whole town knew. Childhood sweethearts, broke up when Sawyer left town on a whim, never really resolved anything. And now here they were, staring at each other like the world might end if either of them moved.

"Yikes..." I cleared my throat. "I should get back to—yeah."

I retreated to the back room before I could make things worse, but I couldn't help hearing Maple's voice carry through: "Daddy, this is the best cookie I've ever had. I'm going to marry this cookie."

Despite everything, I had to bite back a grin. The kid had good taste.

I turned my attention back to the shelves, recalculating measurements and trying to figure out how to make Isla's vision work in the actual space. The sound of hammering kept me company while voices drifted from the front—Maple chattering, Isla's responses careful and measured, Sawyer's awkward attempts at normal conversation.

Twenty minutes later, the bell over the front door chimed. Footsteps retreated. Silence.

"You can come out now," Isla called. "Coast is clear."

I emerged to find her leaning against the counter, arms crossed, staring at the door like she could see through it to wherever Sawyer had gone.

"So," I said. "That was..."

"Don't." She held up a hand. "I don't want to talk about it."

"Wasn't going to." I grabbed my water bottle from where I'd left it near the register. "Though for the record, my niece is adorable."

"She is." Something in Isla's expression softened. "She called me Princess Isla."

"Well, you do run a magic cookie kingdom. Makes sense."

That got a smile, small but genuine. "How are the shelves coming?"

"They're coming. Your measurements were optimistic, but I'll make it work." I took a sip of water. "Might need to adjust the bracket placement, though. And possibly perform minor structural miracles."

"That's why I called you instead of trying to do it myself." She moved to the display case, started rearranging pastries. "You're good at making things work when they shouldn't."

I wasn't sure if that was a compliment or an observation about my entire life, so I just nodded and headed back to the shelves.

My phone buzzed in my tool belt. Then again. Then three more times in rapid succession.

I ignored it. Whatever it was could wait until I finished marking the bracket holes. The buzzing continued—five more notifications in the span of thirty seconds. Either someone had died or—

"Are you going to answer that?" Isla's voice came from the doorway. "Because whoever it is seems persistent."

"It's probably nothing." I set down my pencil and pulled out my phone.

Twelve messages. All from Quinn Fairchild. All sent between 6:15 and 6:47 a.m.

I stared at the screen, my thumb hovering over the notification. We'd been assigned to work together yesterday at the town meeting. She'd seemed nice. Enthusiastic. The kind of person who probably didn't understand that most people weren't fully functional before seven a.m.

"Nothing?" Isla raised an eyebrow. "Your face says it's definitely something."

"It's the festival booth assignment. Quinn Fairchild."

"The costume shop owner?" Isla's mouth curved. "Aunt Caroline mentioned you two got paired up. How convenient."

"Not you too." I opened the message thread, scrolling through Quinn's early morning enthusiasm. "Mayor Goldwin needed someone to help with the booth and I was sitting there. That's all."

"Uh huh." Isla disappeared back into the front, but I could hear the amusement in her voice. "Sure it is."

I focused on the messages.

> Couldn't sleep so I sketched some backdrop
> ideas! What do you think of a vintage
> carnival theme?

The attached sketch was detailed—striped carnival tent with fairy lights and hand-painted signage. The proportions were slightly off, but the concept was solid. She'd included period-accurate details most people wouldn't bother with.

I scrolled through the rest. Color swatches. Mood boards. Three different angles. A Pinterest board with 147 pins.

> Okay I know I'm being A LOT but I'm just
> really excited about this! Carnival + Victorian
> Gothic = PERFECT Halloween vibes, right?

> Sorry if I woke you. Or if you're not a
> morning person. Or if you think I'm
> completely unhinged for texting this much
> about a photo booth.

> I'll stop now. Maybe. Probably not. But
> I'll try!

Three exclamation points in the last message. The woman used punctuation like other people used confetti.

My phone buzzed again. Another photo—a ridiculous feathered hat, bright purple with plumes extending at least two feet in every direction.

> Is this too much? (Trick question—it's
> definitely too much. But is it TOO too
> much?)

I stared at the photo. She was holding the hat up to the camera, and I could see part of her face behind it. Her mouth curved in a grin, one eyebrow raised like she was in on the joke.

My mouth twitched before I could stop it.

I started typing: *That hat could be seen from space. Possibly from other planets.*

My thumb hovered over send. This was a response that would encourage more texts. More photos. More of her personality filling up my phone and making me check it every ten minutes.

I deleted it and typed something else.

> Looks good. Let me know what you need.

Professional. Brief. Exactly what I should have sent.

My phone rang immediately.

Quinn's name flashed across the screen and my stomach dropped. We'd been assigned to work together yesterday. She'd sent me fifteen texts. That did not constitute a phone call relationship.

But she might keep calling if I didn't answer.

I hit accept. "Yeah?"

"Oh good, you're alive!" Her voice was bright, slightly breathless. "I was starting to think my texts were going into some kind of void. Do you have a minute? I have ideas."

"I'm working."

"Right, of course." She didn't sound discouraged. In the background, I could hear fabric rustling. "But just really quick—I was thinking about the carnival theme versus Victorian Gothic, and I think we could actually combine them. Hear me out."

She didn't wait for me to respond. Words tumbled over each other, and I stepped out of the back room, through the kitchen, and out into the alley behind the bakery where Isla wouldn't overhear.

"What if we did vintage Halloween carnival aesthetic? Like, creepy-cute? Victorian silhouettes but with carnival stripes, and we could use those old-fashioned circus fonts for the signage, and—are you still there?"

"I'm here."

"Okay good, because I'm not done. So the color palette would be burgundy and gold, cream and forest green—very autumn, very theatrical—and I found this incredible bolt of velvet at the fabric store in the next town over, which would be perfect for draping. Very dramatic but also seasonal, you know?"

I did know. I could see it already—the way heavy velvet would photograph, how it would frame the booth, the exact shade of burgundy that would complement autumn lighting.

"The owner said she'd give me a discount if we mentioned her shop in the festival program," Quinn continued, "so that's built-in partnership potential, and—"

"That could work." The words escaped before I could stop them.

She paused. "Really?"

"The aesthetic. Vintage carnival meets Victorian Gothic. It's different enough to stand out but still seasonal." I leaned against the wall, already seeing the design. "You'd need to balance the elements carefully though. Too much carnival and it reads childish. Too much Gothic and it's Spirit Halloween knockoff."

"Yes! Exactly!" The enthusiasm in her voice ratcheted up. "That's what I was thinking, but I couldn't articulate it that way. You just, like, immediately got it."

My chest tightened. I pressed my palm against the brick wall, focusing on the texture.

"The signage would be important," I continued, not sure why I was still talking. "Hand-painted, probably. Nothing printed or commercial looking. And the lighting needs to feel like old carnival bulbs, not modern LEDs."

"I have vintage bulbs! Or, well, reproduction vintage bulbs that look old-fashioned." She was definitely walking now. I could hear her footsteps. "Oh, and I was thinking about props. Not just hats and boas, but specific pieces that tell stories. Like a fortune teller's crystal ball, or a ringmaster's hat, or—"

"A strongman's weights," I said. "Fake ones. Painted to look cast iron."

"Yes! Or a sword swallower's prop sword. Oh, this is perfect." She laughed, and the sound was loud and completely unself-conscious. My hand stilled against the brick. "We should meet before Saturday. Thursday, maybe? At the shop? I want to show you the space and we can start sketching actual plans of the booth instead of just texting ideas into the void."

Thursday. That was two days away.

"I have jobs Thursday morning," I said.

"Morning and afternoon?"

"Morning." I stopped, because what came next felt like admitting something. I usually used Thursday afternoons for catching up on paperwork and supply runs, but nothing about that was urgent enough to justify saying no.

"Afternoon then?" She pressed on, hopeful. "Three o'clock? I'm flexible. The shop's closed Wednesdays anyway so I'll be doing inventory all day tomorrow, which means Thursday I'll be desperate for human interaction and creative collaboration." She paused for breath. "Unless you'd rather wait until Saturday like we originally planned, which is totally fine, I'm just excited and getting ahead of myself, which I do, it's a problem—"

"Thursday at three." The words came out before I'd decided to say them.

Silence on the other end, just for a beat. Then: "Perfect. Okay. Great. I'll text you the address, but it's just Main Street, the purple door; you literally can't miss it. And I'll pull together some physical samples so we're not just looking at phone screens. This is going to be amazing, Asher. I can feel it."

She hung up before I could respond, leaving me standing in the alley with my phone in my hand and the uncomfortable knowledge that I'd just agreed to meet with her two days earlier than necessary.

I headed back inside. Isla was at the counter, boxing up an order, but she looked up when I entered.

"Everything okay?"

"Yeah. Fine." I grabbed my tools. "Just planning the booth setup."

"Uh huh." She handed the box to a customer, then turned back to me. "You know, when people plan festival booths, they usually don't look quite so..."

"So what?"

"Conflicted." She was fighting a smile. "Like they're not sure if they've just made the best or worst decision of their life."

"It's just a booth," I said, heading back to the shelves. "The mayor said I should help, so I'm helping. It's just a collaboration. Nothing complicated."

"Right. Not complicated at all."

I ignored her and focused on the brackets, but my phone kept buzzing. Quinn sending the address. Then asking about coffee preferences. Then mentioning cookies from the bakery down the street; the very bakery in which I stood.

> Sorry, I know I'm being a lot. My ex used to say I was exhausting. But I promise I'll try to be normal on Thursday. Well, normal-ish. Okay probably not normal at all, but I'll bring good cookies as compensation.

The mention of her ex made something sharp lodge in my throat. Someone had called her exhausting. Had made her apologize for her enthusiasm.

I responded.

> Coffee's fine. See you Thursday.

Then, before I could overthink it, I added something I probably shouldn't have.

> And you're not exhausting.

I sent it and immediately wished I could take it back. Too personal. Too encouraging.

Three dots appeared. Disappeared. Appeared again.

> Thank you for saying that. :)

A smiley face.

"Asher?" Isla's voice came from the doorway. "How much longer do you think you'll need? I have to run to a supplier before they close."

"Another hour, maybe." I set down my drill. "I can lock up when I'm done if you trust me with the keys."

"Of course I trust you." She grabbed her purse and jacket. "Just don't burn the place down."

"No promises."

She laughed and headed out, leaving me alone in the bakery with the smell of cinnamon and fresh bread and the weight of Quinn's sideways smile in my pocket.

I finished the shelves by noon, cleaning up my tools and sweeping the sawdust. The front of the bakery was quiet, afternoon sun slanting through the windows, making everything look warm and golden.

My phone vibrated.

I told myself I wouldn't check it. Told myself I needed to maintain distance, keep things professional.

I checked it anyway.

A video. Quinn wearing that ridiculous purple-feathered hat from earlier, standing in front of a full-length mirror. She was laughing as she adjusted it, completely unrestrained, like she'd forgotten the camera was there.

I watched it loop. Once. Twice. The way she wrinkled her nose when the feathers tickled her face. The paint smudge on her forearm. The unselfconscious joy.

My thumb moved to reply: *That hat has its own gravitational field.*
Deleted it. Too familiar.

Tried again: *Looks period-appropriate for 1920s showgirl aesthetic.*
Too stiff.

Finally settled.

> See you Thursday.

Safe. Professional.

I locked up the bakery and headed to my truck, already thinking about the afternoon's jobs. Mrs. Hawthorne needed her back step fixed. The Jones's fence was still waiting on parts. Normal, practical work that didn't involve thinking about purple feathers.

That determination lasted until I got to Mrs. Hawthorne's house and sketched carnival tent designs on the back of my work order while I waited for the concrete to set.

The proportions were better than Quinn's version—the stripes narrower, more authentic to actual 1920s carnival tents. I studied it for a moment, then crumpled the paper and shoved it in my pocket.

Not practical. Not helpful. Just another reminder that I'd chosen handyman work over art school when Dad had his heart attack, because someone had to be practical and Levi was already managing the farm and Sawyer had left to who knew where.

My phone vibrated.

> I'm already excited for Thursday! Fair warning, I've been collecting prop ideas and I might have gone overboard. Also I found three more color swatches that would be PERFECT. Also I have nineteen questions about lighting. Is that too many questions? That's probably too many questions. I'll try to narrow it down to ten. Maybe twelve.

I stared at the message, my mouth doing that traitorous almost-smile thing again.

Nineteen questions about lighting.

My thumb moved to reply. I should keep it brief. Something like "Sounds good."

> Nineteen seems reasonable. Bring all nineteen.

I sent it before I could reconsider.

Three dots appeared immediately.

> Really? You're not going to run screaming? Because people usually run screaming when I start talking about gels and spotlights and ambient versus direct lighting.

> This is going to be so fun!!! Thursday can't come fast enough!

Three exclamation points. Again.

I pocketed my phone and finished Mrs. Hawthorne's step, telling myself the lightness in my chest was just satisfaction at having a plan.

Not anticipation. Not the dangerous flutter of possibility. Not the unwelcome awareness that Thursday at three o'clock suddenly felt very far away.

But that night, lying in bed in my apartment above Art's hardware store, I pulled out my phone one last time. Opened Quinn's contact information. Stared at her name.

Then I added a small purple heart emoji next to it. Ridiculous. Impulsive. The kind of thing teenagers did. I saved it anyway.

Thursday at three o'clock was still two days away, but somehow, lying there in the dark, it felt both too far away and not nearly far enough.

# Chapter Three

### QUINN

Thursday afternoon arrived with perfect October light streaming through my shop windows, turning dust motes into tiny dancers and making the velvet fabric I'd been rearranging glow like spilled wine.

The truck engine cut off outside, and my stomach flipped. I was far too excited. Carter would've told me to calm down and take some deep breaths, but he wasn't there. So instead, I bounced on the balls of my feet and waited.

Through the window, I watched Asher climb out—flannel shirt rolled to his elbows, work boots, jeans with paint stains mapping out previous projects. He checked his phone before heading toward my door, and I used those five seconds to smooth my sweater and try to convince myself this was just a fun fall collaboration with a guy who was unfairly attractive and also listened when I talked instead of waiting for me to stop.

My shop looked like a craft store had a nervous breakdown. Fabric draped over every available surface. Sketches papered the walls with no organizational system beyond "things I liked" and "things I might like later." Half-finished costume pieces hung from racks like optimistic ghosts. The Victorian fainting couch was buried under ribbon spools.

My worktable could charitably be described as "actively creative" and less charitably as "intervention-worthy."

You're too scattered, Carter's voice whispered. This is why you never finish anything.

I shoved the thought away. Organized people didn't run successful custom costume businesses out of small-town shops, did they? Well, actually they probably did, but I was making it work my own way, thank you very much.

The bell above my door chimed at exactly three o'clock.

Asher stood in my doorway, and I braced myself for the reaction I'd gotten from Carter the first time he'd seen my workspace; the tight smile, the careful "it's very you" that meant "this is chaos and you should be embarrassed."

But Asher was already walking toward the wall where I'd tacked up my festival booth sketches, studying them with that focused intensity I'd noticed at the town meeting. His head tilted slightly as he examined the carnival tent version, then moved to the Victorian Gothic design, eyes tracking every line.

"Hi," I said, too bright. "Come in. Sorry about the mess. I was working on a commission and things got a little—anyway, there's coffee and cookies like I promised—"

"These are good," he said without looking away from my sketches.

I twisted the hem of my sweater between my fingers. "Really? Because I know the proportions are probably off, and the color balance needs work, and the perspective on this one makes the whole thing look lopsided—"

"They're good." He pointed to my carnival tent sketch. "The concept is solid. But this stripe pattern would be difficult to paint at scale without looking muddy from a distance. You'd want to simplify the design here and here." His finger traced the areas, and I noticed his hands again—long fingers with calluses at the base of his palm, paint stains in forest green along one thumbnail. "And the lighting placement would create shadows across the main backdrop. You'd need to shift the angle or people's photos would have dark spots across their faces."

He was right. Completely right. I could see it now, the way the stripes would blur together from fifteen feet away, how the shadows would ruin the whole effect.

"That's annoying," I said.

The corner of his mouth lifted. Almost a smile, which somehow felt like winning something. "What is?"

"That you're right. I spent two hours on those sketches yesterday and you just—" I gestured at the wall. "Walked in and immediately saw the problems I couldn't."

"I've had practice. Made plenty of mistakes on signs over the years." He moved to the next sketch—my Victorian Gothic version with its dramatic silhouettes and moody color palette. "This one's stronger technically but less distinctive. Everyone does Gothic Halloween. The carnival combination makes yours memorable."

I grabbed my sketchbook from the worktable, pages already marked with coffee rings and pencil smudges, corners bent from being shoved in my bag. "So what if we merged them? Keep the carnival stripes but use Victorian silhouettes as the main focal points instead of competing elements?"

Asher took the sketchbook from my hands, and our fingers brushed —barely a second of contact—but warmth shot up my arm and settled somewhere behind my ribs. I pulled back too fast, knocked my hip into the worktable, and sent a stack of fabric samples cascading onto the floor.

"Sorry, I'm—let me just—" I crouched to gather the fallen fabric, heat creeping up my neck. Very professional. Very coordinated. Carter would have that pinched expression he got when I knocked things over, the one that said "why can't you be more careful?"

When I stood, Asher was studying my sketch with complete focus, like nothing else existed. He didn't acknowledge my clumsiness, didn't make it a thing. Just kept examining my work with those careful eyes.

"This could work," he said after a long moment. "The contrast would photograph well. You'd need to be careful with the color palette though—too many competing elements and it reads busy instead of intentional."

"Right. Intentional." I was talking too fast, filling space while he processed. I bit my lip and made myself wait, count to five before speaking again.

Asher looked up after maybe three seconds. "Coffee?"

"Yes. Coffee. I have coffee." I fled to the small kitchenette, grateful for something to do with my hands. The coffee was still hot—pumpkin spice, because I was apparently committed to every fall cliché this town had to offer. I filled two mismatched vintage mugs and carried them back to find Asher at my worktable, already sketching on a blank piece of paper with one of my pencils.

"Here." I set his mug down carefully, catching the scent of soap and hay and something woodsy when I leaned close. The same scent from the town meeting, but stronger now in my small shop where the air didn't have anywhere else to go.

"Thanks." He slid the paper toward me without looking up. "Layout concept. Combining your ideas with a few adjustments. You can tell me if you hate it."

I moved to stand beside him, close enough to see the way he held the pencil, the confidence in each line. He'd taken my concept and refined it —showing exactly how the carnival stripes would frame Victorian silhouettes, where props would be placed for traffic flow, how lighting angles would eliminate unwanted shadows. His fixes elevated my vision into something that could actually exist in three dimensions.

"This is incredible," I mumbled.

"It's your design. I just adjusted the execution." He added shading to one corner, demonstrating depth. "What if we went with burgundy and gold instead of traditional orange and black? More Victorian carnival than modern Halloween."

I grabbed a red marker from the table. "Yes, and we could add vintage carnival game elements here—like a ring toss or bottle pyramid, but styled Gothic with tarnished gold details."

Asher picked up a green marker. "Black base with gold accents would pop against burgundy."

We both reached for the same spot on the paper.

Our hands collided. His fingers landed over mine—callused, warm, paint-stained. I froze. The contact sent warmth racing up my arm, made my breath catch in a way that had nothing to do with festival booth planning and everything to do with the way he'd gone completely still, his hand resting over mine like he'd forgotten how to move.

For three heartbeats, neither of us breathed.

Then I yanked my hand back, nearly knocked over my coffee mug in the process, and grabbed for it with both hands. Asher's hand shot out at the same time, and we caught the mug together, his palm warm against the back of my hand, steadying the cup between us.

"That was close," I managed, voice higher than normal.

"Yeah." His voice was rougher. He dragged his hand away. "Sorry. Should've paid attention to where you were reaching."

"No, I just—I grabbed without looking." I set the mug down more carefully, hands shaking slightly. "You take the red marker. I can use burgundy."

He picked up the marker, and his hand wasn't quite steady either. "Thanks."

We both stared at the sketch instead of each other, but I could still feel the ghost of his warmth on my knuckles, could hear his breathing slightly uneven in the quiet shop.

"So," I said, voice too bright. "Carnival games. Black base with gold details?"

"Victorian era had carnival games too." He cleared his throat. "We could research period-accurate designs. Make it historically grounded."

"Yes, and maybe old carnival posters as part of the backdrop? I have reproduction posters in storage. Or we could make our own—hand-painted to look vintage but advertising the festival vendors. Very old-timey circus poster language."

"That would tie into the local farms." Asher started sketching again, his hand keeping pace with my words. "Feature different festival vendors. Make it community-focused instead of just decorative."

We fell into a rhythm after that. Me talking through ideas while Asher sketched and refined them, his pencil translating my enthusiastic rambling into architectural drawings. When I went on a tangent about Victorian-era circus performers and how they used dramatic lighting to create illusions, he listened without interrupting and then incorporated the lighting concept into his backdrop design. When I changed my mind about color placement for the third time, he adjusted without complaint, just erased and redrew like it was the most natural thing in the world.

An hour disappeared into creative collaboration that felt easier than breathing.

The afternoon light shifted across my worktable, turning from bright white to warm gold. The smell of old fabric mixed with coffee and the faint scent of paint on Asher's clothes. From outside, Main Street settled into late afternoon—kids heading home from school, shop doors chiming, someone's car radio playing too loud before fading into the distance.

I grabbed the cookie plate I'd forgotten about and offered it to Asher, watching him take one without interrupting his sketching. We stood side by side at the table, close enough that warmth radiated from him, our arms almost touching every time one of us reached for a different marker.

"Wait," I said, grabbing tracing paper from my supply cabinet. "What if we did layered backdrops? Carnival stripes as the first layer, Victorian silhouettes behind them. The lighting would create depth between the layers instead of everything being flat?"

Asher's hand stilled on his sketch. He looked up at me. "That would create actual dimension. Make it feel immersive instead of just a photo background."

"Exactly! And we could have some silhouettes in front too, framing the photo space, so people are literally standing inside the design instead of just in front of it."

He was already sketching it, his pencil moving faster now. "Three distinct planes. Front frame, middle photo space, background depth. Lighting positioned to highlight each layer separately without washing out the others." He looked up again, and this time he almost smiled—a real smile that transformed his entire face from serious to something softer. "That's brilliant."

The praise made warmth flood through my chest. "It just came to me while you were talking about sightlines, and I started thinking about theater set design and how Victorian stages used forced perspective tricks to create depth, and there's this whole history of painted backdrops that made small stages look enormous, and—sorry, I'm rambling."

"Keep going," he interrupted, but gently. "That tangent just solved our biggest design problem."

I blinked at him. "Really?"

"Really."

"Right. Okay. So Victorian theaters used painted perspective to make small stages look enormous, and they'd layer set pieces at different depths with lighting to enhance the illusion—" I was using my hands now, gesturing to illustrate the concept, completely in my element. "And if we apply that same principle but with modern materials and LED lighting, we could create depth that photographs beautifully while still being structurally simple enough to build in a couple weeks."

Asher kept sketching. His pencil moved across the paper, adding notes about materials and measurements, building on my ideas instead of trying to organize them into something more manageable.

We worked for another hour, the collaboration flowing so naturally I forgot to second-guess myself. I kept catching myself about to apologize for talking too much, for changing my mind, for going off on tangents. But Asher never looked annoyed. He just kept up, occasionally asking clarifying questions or suggesting technical improvements that elevated my vision without changing its core.

The light outside shifted to amber, and the temperature started dropping the way it did in early October when afternoon gave way to evening. I pulled on the cardigan I kept on my desk chair, and Asher rolled down his sleeves without commenting on the time.

"This is the best collaboration I've had in years," I said, studying our final sketches spread across the table—three distinct design iterations showing our evolution from competing concepts to merged brilliance. "My ex used to say I was too scattered. That I needed to focus. But look, we made something really cool even with scatterbrained thoughts."

Asher's hand stilled on the paper. His jaw tightened, and something fierce crossed his face before his expression went carefully neutral. He set down his marker like he was trying to control something.

"You're not scatterbrained."

"Thanks, but I know I'm exhausting," I continued, the words spilling out before I could stop them. "My creative process is chaos pretending to be productivity." I was making it worse, explaining when I should drop it, but I couldn't seem to stop. "My ex had systems. Organization. Project management software. Said if I could just organize my thoughts before speaking, present finished ideas instead of thinking out loud, I'd be more effective."

Asher's hands curled into fists at his sides. The late afternoon light from the window caught his profile—the scar through his eyebrow, the paint stains on his collar, the exact shade of gray-green in his eyes that reminded me of sage leaves.

"Your process isn't chaos," he said finally, voice rough with something that sounded like anger on my behalf. "It's how you think. Out loud, building on ideas, making connections other people wouldn't see because they're too busy following predetermined systems." He gestured at the sketches covering the table. "This happened because you talked through every possibility. If you'd organized your thoughts first and only shared the finished version, we'd have something boring and predictable that looked like every other festival booth."

My chest tightened. I pressed my palms against the worktable edge, needing something solid under my hands.

"And you're not exhausting." His eyebrows drew together, jaw working like he was testing words before speaking them. "Your ex was probably just too rigid to keep up with you. Too small to handle who you are. Not your fault he couldn't keep up. That's his limitation, not yours."

The shop went very quiet. I could hear my heartbeat, the old radiator ticking in the corner, the distant sound of someone closing up their shop on Main Street.

"Oh," I managed, throat too tight for anything else.

My phone buzzed on the worktable between us. Carter's name lit up the screen.

I reached for it automatically, then stopped. Let it ring. The sound felt invasive in the comfortable silence Asher and I had built, like Carter was reaching through the phone.

The ringing stopped. Five seconds of blessed quiet.

Then it started again.

I grabbed the phone and silenced it, shoving it in my cardigan pocket without looking at the screen. "Sorry. He's persistent."

Asher's jaw tightened further, but he didn't ask. Just watched me with those careful eyes, seeing more than I wanted him to.

"He calls sometimes," I said, trying to make it sound casual. "Wants to 'check in' even though we've been broken up a while. I should probably just block him."

"Probably," Asher agreed, voice flat.

The shop bell chimed, making us both jump.

Aunt Caroline stood in my doorway, holding a covered dish and taking in the scene with bright eyes. Our sketches spread across the table, two coffee mugs, the way we'd been standing close enough to share warmth.

"Don't mind me," she said, smiling. "Just dropping off some left-over pie for you, Quinn. Thought you might want a snack while you're working so hard."

"Oh, thank you! That's so thoughtful—"

"Asher." Aunt Caroline set the pie on my counter, taking her time, clearly assessing everything. "Didn't expect to see you here."

"Festival booth planning," he said, voice carefully neutral.

"Mm-hmm." She adjusted the dish cover unnecessarily. "Looks like you two are making good progress."

"We are," I offered, gesturing at the table. "Combining Victorian and carnival elements with layered backdrops."

"That sounds lovely." Aunt Caroline headed toward the door. "Well, don't let me interrupt your work. You both look very focused."

She left, and I waited until the bell stopped chiming before turning to Asher. "She's going to tell everyone, isn't she?"

"Probably already composing the text." The corner of his mouth lifted. "Small towns."

"Does that bother you? The gossip thing?"

"Grew up here. You get used to people being interested in your business. Besides, she's my aunt." He added final details to one of the silhouettes. "Does it bother you?"

"I don't know yet. Still figuring out if I belong here or if I'm just passing through." The admission slipped out before I could stop it, more honest than I'd meant to be.

Asher's pencil paused. He looked at me for a long moment, something unreadable in his expression. "You've been here three months. Give it time."

"Is that how long it took you? Three months to know you belonged?"

"I was born here. Never had to figure it out." He went back to sketching, but I caught the slight tension in his shoulders. "Left for college, came back because my oldest brother Levi needed help with the farm. Wasn't really a choice."

"Do you regret coming back?"

"No." The answer came quickly, certain. "This valley matters. These people matter. Building something that lasts here—that matters more than whatever I thought I wanted somewhere else."

"Where did you learn to draw?" I asked.

He stilled, took a deep breath, and then glanced at me. "My mom started me on it when I was young. She liked painting. I tried it, but haven't done it in a while."

"Painting? I bet you're wonderful at it!" I glanced over my shoulder at the door that led to the back room, furrowing my brows. "I have an easel. Maybe you could come here and paint sometime?"

"No."

"Oh. Right. Sorry, I didn't mean to—"

"Don't apologize. It's just that I haven't painted in a really long time and I wouldn't be good at it anymore." He softened his voice, but didn't look at me.

"Well, if you ever change your mind, I'd love to watch you." I paused, and then realized how creepy that sounded. "Not in a weird way. Just in a, I don't know, painting way. If that makes sense."

He did look at me then, raising an eyebrow. "A painting way?"

"Nevermind. Let's finish this, shall we?" Gesturing towards the table, I prayed the flush hadn't reached my cheeks. I grabbed a burgundy marker and added final color notes to our sketch, using the motion to cover my sudden nervousness about the way this conversation was heading toward things that felt important.

We worked for another thirty minutes, the light outside fading to deep purple, the shop growing colder as the October evening settled in. I turned on my vintage lamps, casting warm circles of light across our worktable, and Asher didn't mention leaving even though it was past dinner time.

"I should go," he said finally, checking his phone. "I've got some jobs to prepare for tomorrow morning."

"Right. Of course." I followed him to the door, my brain already spinning through when we could meet again, how soon I could see him and continue this collaboration that felt like more than just festival planning. "This was really productive. Thank you for—for everything you said. About my process."

Asher paused with his hand on the door, looking back at me. The lamp behind me cast his face in shadow, but I could still see the exact moment he decided to say something else, the way his expression shifted from careful to honest.

"Quinn."

"Yeah?"

"You're not too much." His voice was rough, almost awkward, like the words didn't come easily but he needed to say them anyway. "Don't make yourself smaller because someone else couldn't handle who you are."

Then he was gone, the bell chiming behind him, leaving me standing frozen in the doorway with my hand pressed against my suddenly warm cheek.

I watched through the window as he climbed into his truck, my mind replaying his words on a loop. *You're not too much. Don't make yourself smaller.*

It terrified me, how much those words sounded familiar.

Because Carter had been supportive at first too. Interested in my costume business, encouraging about my ideas, full of compliments. The criticism came later. Small suggestions that grew into constant corrections that grew into me doubting every creative instinct I had. *Just trying to help you be your best self*, he'd say, while dismantling my confidence until I couldn't remember what my best self even looked like.

What if Asher was the same? What if this was just the honeymoon phase before he started finding my enthusiasm annoying, my process exhausting, my personality too much to handle long-term?

My phone buzzed again.

> Forgot to ask - when can we meet to buy materials? Tomorrow too soon?

My fingers hovered over the keyboard. Tomorrow. Less than twenty-four hours until I'd see him again, until I'd have to figure out if this feeling racing through my chest was real or if I was just desperate to believe someone could appreciate my chaos without wanting to fix it.

But I thought about the way he'd listened to my tangents without cutting me off. The way he'd built on my ideas instead of editing them down. The fierce expression on his face when I'd mentioned Carter, like he was angry on my behalf for things I'd convinced myself I deserved.

> Tomorrow works. 10am?

> See you then.

Three words. But they felt like a promise, like the beginning of something that could either heal me or break me worse than Carter ever had.

I pulled out my sketchbook and flipped to a fresh page, intending to draft material lists and measurements. But my hand moved on its own, sketching carnival stripes and Victorian frames and layered backdrops. And in the corner, almost without meaning to, I drew a figure with broad shoulders and paint-stained jeans, holding a pencil with those careful hands.

I stared at it for a long moment, chest tight with want and fear in equal measure.

Then I tucked the marker Asher had used into my desk drawer—saving it for tomorrow when I'd see him again—and let myself imagine walking into the hardware store together, arguing good-naturedly about paint colors, building something beautiful that would last beyond the festival weekend.

*You're not too much. Don't make yourself smaller.*
I was already counting the hours until I'd see him again.

# Chapter Four

## ASHER

The village green pumpkin carving contest happened every year at the beginning of October. Most people considered it a warm-up for the main festival. This one was a small-scale, community-focused event where half the contestants brought their kids and everyone brought way too much confidence about their carving abilities.

I'd never entered before. Never saw the point.

But this year I'd signed up without telling anyone, and now I sat at my assigned station with a pumpkin the size of a basketball and a set of carving tools I'd borrowed from Levi, trying to remember why I'd thought this was a good idea.

"You actually showed up." Levi appeared at my elbow, coffee in hand. He wore his standard flannel and jeans. "Didn't think you'd go through with it."

"Why wouldn't I?"

"Because you've spent the last three years telling me contests are performative nonsense designed to make people feel inadequate." He grinned and handed me the coffee. "Your words, not mine."

I took the coffee without looking at him. "Maybe I changed my mind."

"Mm-hmm. This wouldn't have anything to do with a certain shop owner who mentioned she was entering, would it?"

Heat crept up my neck. "It's just a pumpkin carving contest."

"Right. And I'm just the guy who happened to check the registration list and notice you signed up thirty seconds after Quinn did." He clapped me on the shoulder. "Have fun. Try not to overthink it."

He left, but not before I caught his knowing smile.

I turned my attention to the pumpkin in front of me, studying its shape and color. The morning sun caught the orange surface, highlighting natural ridges and imperfections. I'd been sketching vine patterns in my notebook for the past week—intricate, detailed, the kind of thing that required steady hands and complete focus.

The kind of thing I used to love doing before I convinced myself art was impractical.

I pulled out my tools and made the first cut.

The smell of pumpkin flesh filled the air as I worked, mixing with the scent of fallen leaves and someone's apple cider from a nearby booth.

I'd been carving for maybe twenty minutes when Quinn arrived.

She rushed up to the registration table in paint-splattered overalls and a cream sweater, her hair twisted up in a messy bun with what looked like a paintbrush shoved through it. She carried a bag that appeared to be half carving tools and half art supplies.

I forced myself to look back at my pumpkin, adding another carefully detailed leaf to the vine pattern I'd started. But when Quinn got assigned to a station three down from mine, close enough that I could hear her muttering to herself, staying focused became significantly harder.

She set up her workspace—tools arranged by size, sketch paper spread out, a thermos of something that smelled like cinnamon tea. She examined her pumpkin from multiple angles, made a few pencil marks, erased them, made new marks.

I added another leaf to my vine and pretended I wasn't watching.

Twenty minutes later, I glanced up to rest my cramping hand and found her in complete flow state. Knife moving confidently, no hesitation, no second-guessing. She'd found her rhythm, and the transformation was something to witness. Her tongue stuck out slightly in concentration, and she'd forgotten to be anxious about whether her design would work.

She must have felt me watching because she looked up.

Our eyes met. Three seconds—long enough for warmth to flood my face, for her mouth to curve in a small smile that made my pulse kick up, for me to completely forget which leaf I'd been working on. Then I looked away too fast and nearly dropped my carving knife.

Focus. Right. I had a pumpkin to carve.

I went back to my vine pattern, but my awareness stayed locked on Quinn three stations down. The way she paused every few minutes to assess her progress. The way she tucked escaped hair behind her ear with the back of her wrist, hands too messy to touch her face. The way she bounced slightly when a cut came out exactly right.

"Uncle Asher!" Maple's voice carried across the green before I saw her. She barreled toward my station with Sawyer following at a more reasonable pace, his expression fond as he watched his daughter's enthusiasm.

"Hey, kiddo." I set down my knife as she reached me, her small hands immediately reaching for my pumpkin. "Careful—it's not finished."

"It's so pretty!" She peered at the vine pattern with wide eyes. "Like a fancy garden. Can I help?"

"This one's all mine. But I bet we can find you a pumpkin to carve later."

"With a princess face?"

"Whatever you want."

Sawyer ruffled her hair, then studied my carving with raised eyebrows. "That's actually impressive. Didn't know you could do detailed work like that."

"It's just vine patterns."

"It's more than that." He tilted his head, examining the leaves I'd already completed. "You sketched this out first?"

"Yeah."

"Huh." Something shifted in his expression. "Forgot you used to draw. This is good, Ash."

"Thanks."

"Daddy, can we go see the lady with the sparkly pumpkin?" Maple tugged on Sawyer's hand, pointing toward Quinn's station.

I followed her finger and saw Quinn step back from her pumpkin, assessment clear on her face. Even from here, I could tell something wasn't working with her design.

"Sure thing." Sawyer let Maple drag him toward Quinn's station, then glanced back at me. "You coming?"

I shouldn't. I should stay here and finish my own carving. But my feet were already moving, following them across the grass.

Quinn looked up as we approached, and the frustration on her face gave way to a smile when she saw Maple.

"Well hello! Are you my official judge?"

"Your pumpkin is sparkly!" Maple bounced on her toes. "Can I touch it?"

"Maple." Sawyer's voice held gentle warning. "What do we ask first?"

"Please may I touch your sparkly pumpkin?"

"Absolutely." Quinn gestured to her carving, which I could now see was an ambitious Victorian postcard design—elaborate lettering spelling "Season's Greetings from Acorn Field Heights" surrounded by jack-o-lanterns and autumn leaves. The execution was technically impressive, but something about the composition wasn't quite working. Too much detail in the top half, not enough balance in the bottom.

Maple reached out to trace one of the carved jack-o-lanterns with a careful finger. "It's the most beautiful pumpkin ever."

"You think so?" Quinn's smile turned genuine, the frustration melting away. "That's very kind of you."

My niece was already distracted by something else. Or rather, someone else. "Daddy look! It's Miss Isla. Let's go say hi!" She ran off and Sawyer muttered something under his breath before giving me a small salute and nodding to Quinn.

"What do you think?" Quinn asked me.

"I think he's in love," I mumbled, watching my brother scratch the back of his neck as he started speaking to the town's favorite baker.

"You think my pumpkin's in love?" Quinn teased, and I glanced back at her.

"What? No. My brother is... Anyway." I studied her carving more carefully. The technique was excellent—clean lines, precise cuts—but she'd tried to fit too much into the composition. "The lettering's really good."

"The lettering's about the only thing that is good." She picked up her carving knife, made one cut, then set it down again with a sigh. "I sketched this out five times and it looked perfect on paper. On an actual pumpkin? Not so much."

"The proportions are different," I said before I could stop myself. "Paper's flat. Pumpkins curve. You have to adjust for the three-dimensional surface."

"I know you're right, but I think it's a bit too late at this point." She examined her design. "The bottom half needs more detail to balance the top, but I've already carved so much up here that adding more below will make it too busy."

"Not necessarily." I picked up one of her tools—a smaller blade meant for detailed work. "Could add shadow patterns behind the existing elements. Create depth without adding new shapes."

"Show me?"

I shouldn't. This was a contest. Helping her was probably against the rules.

"Here." I made a few small demonstration cuts in the negative space behind one of her carved jack-o-lanterns, creating the illusion of shadow and depth. "See how that makes the main element pop forward?"

"Oh, yeah. That's perfect. Can you show me how to do that again?"

I demonstrated another section, and she watched. Then she took the tool and tried it herself. The cut came out clean, and she made a small sound of triumph.

"I did it!" She looked up at me, her face bright with excitement, close enough that I could see paint stains on her collar and smell whatever floral soap she used. "Asher, you're a genius."

"It's just shading technique."

"It's brilliant." She went back to her pumpkin, adding shadow patterns to balance her composition. I should return to my own station, but I stayed, watching her work, offering the occasional suggestion when she looked over for feedback.

Somewhere in the process, her hand slipped and caught the bowl with the pumpkin insides.

Slimy orange guts splattered across my shirt.

"Oh my gosh!" Quinn stared at the orange mess on my flannel, her hand flying to her mouth. "I'm so sorry! I didn't mean—my knife just—"

I looked down at my shirt, then at her horrified expression, and something about the whole situation made me laugh. "It's just pumpkin."

"It's all over you!"

"Yeah." I scooped some of the pumpkin guts off my shirt, considering. "Seems only fair to return the favor."

Her eyes went wide. "Asher. Don't you dare."

I took a step closer, pumpkin guts still in hand.

"I said I was sorry!" But she was laughing now, backing away from her station. "That's not—you wouldn't—"

I flicked the pumpkin guts at her.

She shrieked as cold orange slime hit her overalls, then stared at me with a mix of shock and delight. "You did not just do that."

"Seemed only fair."

"Fair?" She grabbed a handful of pumpkin from inside her carving. "I'll show you fair."

What followed was probably not appropriate behavior for a community contest, but neither of us seemed to care. She threw pumpkin guts. I dodged and retaliated. She shrieked with laughter. I tried to maintain dignity and failed completely.

"Children!" Mrs. Oakley called from her station. "Some of us are trying to concentrate!"

We froze, both covered in pumpkin guts, and looked at each other.

Quinn dissolved into laughter first. Silent, shoulder-shaking laughter that made her double over, one hand pressed to her stomach. The sound was infectious, and I laughed too, the kind of deep, genuine laughter I couldn't remember the last time I'd experienced.

"We're a mess," she managed between giggles.

"You started it."

"I did not! My hand slipped!" But she was still laughing, looking at me with eyes bright with amusement. "Truce?"

"Truce."

We cleaned up as best we could with paper towels from the supply station, though we both still smelled distinctly of pumpkin. Quinn's overalls had orange stains that would probably never come out. My shirt was a lost cause. But she kept glancing at me with a smile that made my ribs feel too tight, and I couldn't bring myself to regret any of it.

"I should finish my carving," she said finally, but she didn't move away from where we stood between our stations.

"Yeah. Me too."

Neither of us moved.

Quinn's phone buzzed in her pocket. She pulled it out, glanced at the screen, and her expression shifted—just for a second, something tense crossing her face before she shoved the phone back in her pocket without answering.

"Let me guess, your ex?"

"Yeah." But the ease from a moment ago had vanished, replaced by careful neutrality.

Mayor Goldwin's voice carried across the green. "One hour left, everyone! Final touches!"

Quinn straightened, the moment broken. "Right. Better get back to it."

I returned to my station and tried to focus on my own carving, but my attention kept drifting to Quinn. She'd finished the shadow work I'd suggested, and her pumpkin looked significantly better—still ambitious, maybe too ambitious, but balanced now. Good composition. Strong execution.

She caught me looking and smiled—smaller than before, but genuine.

My chest did that warm thing again.

I forced myself to focus on adding final details to my vine pattern. The leaves needed one more pass to sharpen the edges, and I wanted to add some texture to the stems. Work that required complete concentration, which should have been easy except I kept hearing Quinn's laugh in my head, kept seeing her face light up when the shadow technique worked.

Kept thinking about how her ex called and she didn't answer, but the call made her shoulders tight anyway.

"Time!" Mayor Goldwin called. "Everyone step away from your pumpkins!"

I set down my tools and rolled my shoulders, working out the tension from two hours of hunching over intricate carving work. Around me, other contestants stepped back from their stations, some looking satisfied, others clearly disappointed with their results.

Quinn stood beside her Victorian postcard, and even from here I could see her assessing every detail, cataloging every flaw.

The judges moved through the stations with clipboards, making notes and murmuring assessments. They spent a long time at Quinn's pumpkin, which made her fidget with nervous energy. Spent even longer at mine, which made my palms sweat.

Twenty minutes later, Mayor Goldwin announced the results.

Levi took first place with a perfect jack-o-lantern that somehow looked both traditional and innovative. An elderly woman named Martha took second with an intricate haunted house scene.

Third place went to me.

I stared at the ribbon Mayor Goldwin handed me, trying to process the information. Third place. In a contest I'd only entered because Quinn mentioned she was entering. In something I'd convinced myself was pointless and performative.

"Congratulations, Asher." Mayor Goldwin smiled warmly. "That vine work is exceptional. You have real talent."

"Thank you."

I looked around the green and found Quinn bouncing toward my station, her face bright with enthusiasm.

"Third place!" She reached me and grabbed my arm, completely unselfconscious in her excitement. "Asher, that's incredible! Your first contest and you placed against people who've been doing this for years!"

"You didn't place." The words came out before I could stop them.

"So?" She laughed, completely unbothered. "Mine was way too ambitious for a first attempt. Artistic vision doesn't always translate to

39

vegetables." She gestured at her pumpkin with cheerful acceptance. "But I learned a bunch about three-dimensional design limitations and how to adjust for curved surfaces, so it wasn't a waste. Plus yours was gorgeous and I'm genuinely happy for you."

Her phone buzzed again. This time she pulled it out with reluctance, glanced at the screen, and her expression tightened.

"Ex again?" I asked.

"Yeah." She shoved the phone back in her pocket. "He's called three times today. I don't know what he wants, but I'm not interested in finding out." She forced brightness back into her voice. "Anyway! Are you entering the costume contest at the fall festival? Please tell me you're doing the costume contest."

"I don't really do costumes."

"Of course you don't. Too practical." She rolled her eyes, but she was smiling. "What about the Harvest Moon dance? You have to at least come to that."

"Maybe."

"That's not a no." She bounced slightly, energy returning. "I'm taking that as a yes. Oh! And speaking of the festival..."

She kept talking, enthusiasm spilling out in a rush of words about festival plans and costume ideas and how she'd never been to a real small-town Halloween celebration before. I listened, her face animated with excitement, and felt something settle in my chest.

"Asher?" She'd stopped talking and was looking at me with a slight smile. "You okay? You kind of zoned out there."

"Yeah. Sorry." I shook my head. "Just thinking."

"About?"

"About the festival."

"Good thoughts, I hope?" But before I could answer, she glanced at her watch. "Oh shoot, I need to run. Opening the shop at one and I still need to shower off this pumpkin smell." She started gathering her tools, then paused. "Hey, Asher? That vine carving really is beautiful. You should be proud."

She left in a whirlwind of energy, and I stood at my station holding my third-place ribbon, trying to figure out what had just happened to my emotional distance.

"That girl is a hurricane." Sawyer appeared at my elbow with Maple on his shoulders. "Good kind of hurricane, though."

"She's nice."

"She's interested." He studied my face with that older brother expression that meant he'd figured something out. "And from the way you've been watching her all morning, I'd say it's mutual."

"I wasn't—"

"You threw pumpkin guts at each other. In public. At a community event where half the town was watching." He grinned. "That's either foreplay or a declaration of war, and based on how she looked at you, I'm guessing it's not war."

Heat crept up my neck. "It was just—"

"Don't overthink it." He adjusted Maple on his shoulders. "You like her. She likes you. You're both single adults. Revolutionary concept: maybe just see where it goes?"

"It's not that simple."

"Why not?"

*Because I'm the brother who just helps out. Because I stopped painting three years ago and can't remember how to start again. Because wanting something requires admitting you believe you deserve it, and I'm not sure I do.*

"Because," I said, which wasn't an answer at all.

Sawyer looked at me for a long moment, then sighed. "You know what Mom used to say? 'Practical keeps you alive, but passion makes you live.' She'd want you to do more than just help out and maintain equipment, Ash. She'd want you to actually want something."

I looked away, focusing on my pumpkin instead of his face.

"I should clean up my station."

"Right." He didn't push, which somehow made it worse. "Come on, jellybean. Let's go see if Aunt Caroline has hot cider."

They left, and I stood alone at my station, third-place ribbon in hand, thinking about passion versus practical and which one I'd chosen.

Later, after I'd helped Levi break down the contest stations and watched Quinn's shop lights flicker on across town, I went home and pulled out my old art supplies.

The wooden box lived in the back of my closet, buried under winter coats and boxes of farm receipts. I hadn't touched it since college—hadn't let myself even think about it because wanting something you'd given up only made the loss hurt more.

But I pulled it out anyway.

Inside, brushes I'd collected over years of painting. Tubes of paint in colors I'd mixed myself. Palette knives and rags and all the tools of creation I'd convinced myself I didn't need anymore.

My favorite brush—sable hair that held paint perfectly, the handle worn smooth from my grip—fit my palm like it remembered me. Like the years I hadn't painted were just a pause, not an ending.

I sat on my bedroom floor holding a paintbrush and thinking about the reason I'd put them away in the first place.

Mom believed I could go far with it, and when she died that belief died with her. Picking up a brush after her funeral felt impossible, like trying to create beauty when beauty had been torn from the world. It had been so long now that starting again felt like admitting I'd wasted years being practical instead of living.

I set the brush back in the box carefully and closed the lid. Didn't put it back in the closet though. Left it sitting on my desk where I'd see it every morning.

I picked up my phone and opened a new text to Quinn.

> The mayor asked me to help decorate for the dance. Would you want to help me? I could use your insights.

I stared at the message for a long moment, thumb hovering over send. Then I hit it before I could second-guess myself.

Three dots appeared almost immediately.

> Of course! When?

My fingers shook.

> How about 2 tomorrow?

Perfect. And Asher? I'm really thankful for
your help today.

My third-place ribbon sat on my nightstand, catching moonlight. I picked it up, running my thumb over the smooth fabric, thinking about vine patterns and Victorian postcards and the way Quinn's face had lit up when I placed. About her genuine happiness for my success, her complete lack of ego about losing, her insistence that passion mattered more than practical. Tomorrow couldn't come soon enough.

# Chapter Five

## QUINN

The village green had that quiet, golden quality October afternoons brought—a few dog walkers crossing the grass, shop lights beginning to glow on Main Street, wood smoke drifting from someone's chimney. The gazebo stood white and waiting in the slanted light, and I pulled my wagon of decorations across the lawn, wheels whispering through fallen leaves.

Asher's truck was already parked nearby. I could see him unloading supplies—a ladder, toolbox, coils of wire. He wore flannel in deep burgundy and work boots that had seen actual labor, and something about the capable way he moved made my stomach flip.

"Hey," I called, pulling my wagon the final distance. "I brought decorations."

He turned, and his gaze went to my wagon. "That's a lot."

"I know. I might have gone overboard." Heat crept up my neck. "Do you think it's too much?"

"No." Asher walked over to examine my work, picking up one of the paper lanterns carefully. The evening light caught the intricate cutwork pattern I'd spent hours perfecting. "These are incredible. How long did this take?"

"Um. Maybe twenty hours total? A few weekends ago, I couldn't sleep, so I just kept making things. I was going to use them in the shop, but there's already enough in there."

"I'm impressed." He set the lantern down gently, like it was valuable instead of just paper and glue. "These are going to look amazing up there."

"Oh, thanks."

"Quinn! Asher!" Mayor Goldwin appeared at the edge of the green with his clipboard and his trademark enthusiasm. "Wonderful! The gazebo is going to be the centerpiece of the entire festival. And the Harvest Moon dance will have this place beautifully lit, music playing. Very romantic."

His eyes sparkled between us, and my face heated.

"We'll make it look good," Asher said, already reaching for a garland.

"I have complete faith." Mayor Goldwin beamed. "And don't forget —both of you should attend the dance. Can't miss the fruits of your labor."

He left before either of us could respond, and I busied myself sorting decorations to avoid acknowledging his matchmaking.

We started working, and I expected the usual awkwardness that came with collaborative projects—the negotiation about who did what, the careful dance of not stepping on creative toes. But with Asher, it was easy. He'd hand me wire cutters before I asked. I'd hold the ladder steady without being told. When I reached for the hammer at the same time he set it down, our hands didn't quite touch, but the near-miss sent awareness skittering across my skin.

Twenty minutes in, I realized I'd stopped monitoring myself. No nervous chatter filling quiet spaces. No apologizing for my decoration choices. No second-guessing whether I was being too enthusiastic or too much.

I glanced at Asher, who was carefully securing a lantern. He caught me looking and his mouth curved.

"What?" he asked.

"Nothing. Just—this is nice. Working together without having to perform."

Something shifted in his expression. "You don't have to perform with me."

"I know." And I did know. That was the remarkable part. "That's what makes it nice."

His ears went pink, and we both went back to work, but the silence felt even warmer now.

"Hand me that end?" Asher asked, holding one side of a garland.

I grabbed the other end, and together we stretched it across the gazebo's upper beam. The fabric was heavier than I expected, and I had to step closer to keep it from sagging. Close enough that I could smell his soap—something clean and woodsy.

"Should we drape it like this?" I asked, adjusting my end. "Or more centered?"

"Try it centered first."

I shifted the garland, and we both studied the effect. The centered version looked too formal, stiff against the gazebo's natural charm.

"Actually, I think you were right," Asher said. "The drape gives it more movement."

"Compromise?" I suggested. "Drape on this side, center the next one for balance?"

We tried it, and the combination worked perfectly—structured enough to look intentional, loose enough to feel natural. Asher caught my eye and grinned, and my stomach flipped at the shared victory.

Mrs. Oakley appeared as we were hanging the third garland, carrying a plate wrapped in foil. "Thought you two might need sustenance. Fresh oatmeal cookies."

"You're a lifesaver," I said, gratefully accepting a cookie. The warmth seeped through the foil, and the smell of cinnamon and brown sugar made my mouth water.

"The gazebo looks lovely already." She smiled between us. "Such a nice thing, working together like this."

After she left, Asher handed me a cookie with a slightly exasperated expression. "Everyone in this town has opinions."

"Very strong opinions," I agreed, biting into the cookie. It was perfect—crispy edges, soft center—and I made an appreciative sound.

Asher watched me with an expression I couldn't quite read, then cleared his throat and reached for another garland.

We worked as the sun dropped lower, painting everything gold and amber. I was hanging paper lanterns at varying heights when Maple appeared with Sawyer, her face lighting up when she saw our progress.

"It's so pretty!" She bounced on her toes. "Can I help? Please?"

"Sure," I said. "Want to add these sparkles to the pumpkins?"

I handed her a bag of biodegradable glitter, and she set to work with intense concentration, tongue poking out slightly as she carefully sprinkled shimmer over the fabric pumpkins I'd made. Sawyer gave me an approving thumbs-up.

"That one needs more sparkles," Maple declared, pointing at a pumpkin Asher had just positioned. "Everything needs sparkles."

"Can't argue with that logic, kiddo," Asher said solemnly, and Maple beamed.

The sun was touching the horizon when I climbed the ladder with another garland. Asher stood below, one hand on the ladder's frame, and I stretched up to reach the hook. The evening light turned everything molten—gold bleeding into orange, the white gazebo glowing warm. My fingertips brushed the metal beam, almost there.

"Little higher," Asher said, and I rose on my toes.

The ladder shifted.

Not much—just the slightest wobble—but enough that my stomach dropped and my balance wavered.

Asher's hands landed on my waist.

Immediate. Gentle. His palms spread across my ribs through my sweater, fingers pressing just above my hip bones, and heat bloomed where he touched. I steadied, finding the hook and securing the garland, but his hands stayed. Three heartbeats. Four. His thumbs pressed against my sides, and I could feel each individual finger, the warmth bleeding through cotton, the exact pressure that kept me grounded.

I wasn't falling anymore, but he didn't let go.

Neither of us moved. I could feel my pulse everywhere—throat, wrists, the places where his hands touched. Could feel the shift in his breathing, could sense the moment we both realized this had lasted too long to be just about steadying me.

I stepped down carefully, and his hands slid away like he had to remind himself to release me.

My legs felt unsteady for reasons that had nothing to do with the ladder. I turned to face him, and his ears were pink, his jaw tight, his eyes darker than they'd been a moment ago.

"You okay?" His voice came out rough.

"Yeah." Mine wasn't much better. "Thanks for the catch."

"Anytime."

We both turned away at the same moment, reaching for different supplies, putting careful distance between us. But my waist still felt warm where his hands had been, and I kept losing my train of thought.

We were hanging the final decorations when Mayor Goldwin returned to inspect our progress.

"Magnificent!" He climbed the gazebo steps, surveying everything with visible delight. "You two make quite the team. The dance is going to be absolutely magical here."

"Thanks," I managed, hyperaware of Asher standing close enough that our shoulders almost touched.

"Such beautiful work deserves to be celebrated." Mayor Goldwin's smile turned knowing. "Both of you should come dance in the space you've created."

My face heated. "We'll see."

"Of course, of course." His expression said he'd already decided we'd be there together. He left with a wink.

I was gathering empty boxes when my phone buzzed in my pocket. Then buzzed again.

I ignored it, focusing on folding cardboard.

The phone rang.

"You can get that," Asher said, securing the final lantern.

"It's fine." But I pulled out my phone to silence it, and Carter's name flashed across the screen.

My entire body went rigid.

I hit decline, and immediately a text appeared.

> Hey Quinn, just checking in. Hope you're settling in okay up there.

I stared at the words, throat tight. The message looked friendly. Concerned. Exactly the tone Carter used when he wanted something.

Another text.

> I've been thinking about you. About us. Miss talking to you.

Delete.

> I know things ended badly, but we invested two years together. That means something.

Delete.

Another message appeared before I could put the phone away.

> I'm worried about your financial situation. Starting a business is risky. I could help if you need it.

My hands shook. He'd phrased it as concern, but underneath was the same message he'd been sending for weeks: *You can't do this without me. You'll fail and come back.*

One more text.

> Planning to visit in a few weeks. Would love to catch up, no pressure. Just talk.

The phone nearly slipped from my fingers. Carter. Here. In the safe space I'd been building piece by piece.

"Quinn."

I looked up to find Asher watching me, concern mixed with something harder in his expression.

"You okay?" he asked carefully.

"Fine. Just—" I forced a smile that felt brittle. "My ex. He keeps texting. It's annoying."

"What's he saying?"

"That he wants to talk. That he's worried about me. That he might

49

visit." The words came out bitter. "He won't accept that I ended things. Keeps trying to find reasons we need to stay in contact."

Asher's jaw tightened, and his hands flexed at his sides before he deliberately relaxed them. "Have you told him to stop?"

"Multiple times." I wrapped my arms around myself. "He's not dangerous or anything. Just persistent. He thinks if he's nice enough, patient enough, I'll realize I made a mistake and come back."

"That's not being nice. That's not respecting your boundaries."

"I know," I mumbled. "But he's careful. Everything he says sounds reasonable if you don't know the context."

My phone buzzed again. I looked at the screen and saw another message.

> Just want to make sure you're okay. You know I care about you.

I shoved the phone into my pocket without responding.

"Quinn." Asher stepped closer. "If you need anything. I'm here."

"Thank you, but I'm fine. Really."

We finished packing supplies in silence that felt heavier than comfortable. The gazebo glowed in the twilight, beautiful and magical, but Carter's texts had stained the evening.

I loaded my wagon, and Asher walked me to my car.

"Tomorrow at three?" he asked. "Shop visit to talk about your booth?"

"Yeah." I managed a real smile this time. "I'll have supplies ready."

"Good." He hesitated, like he wanted to say more, then just squeezed my shoulder gently. "Drive safe."

The drive home passed in a blur of streetlights and darkening sky. I kept checking my rearview mirror for headlights that followed too close, for any sign that Carter's visit might be sooner than "a few weeks." By the time I parked outside my cottage, my shoulders ached from tension.

Inside, I made tea I couldn't drink and sat on my couch with my phone face-down on the cushion beside me. What would I do when Carter showed up? Hide? Pretend I wasn't there? Watch him charm Mayor Goldwin, playing the concerned ex just trying to help?

And Asher. He'd see me shrink and apologize and second-guess every word. Would see the person Carter had made me instead of the person I was becoming.

My phone buzzed, and my heart lurched—

But it was Asher.

Gazebo looks good.

Relief flooded through me so intensely I had to close my eyes. He'd texted. After I'd shut down, after the awkwardness of Carter's interruption, he'd still reached out with something normal.

Thanks again for today. Sorry about the ending.

Three dots appeared. Disappeared.

Don't apologize. Just... if you need anything, you know where to find me. And, I was thinking, maybe I'd take you up on that painting offer?

I stared at the message, throat tight. Support without pushing. Space while making sure I knew he was there. Everything Carter had never been.

Tomorrow at 3?

I'll be there.

I set my phone down and touched my waist where his hands had been, remembering the warmth that had bloomed under his palms, the way time had stretched in that moment, the feeling that something had shifted between us.

Carter was planning to visit Acorn Field Heights. But tomorrow, Asher would be in my shop. I pulled my favorite blanket around my shoulders and let myself imagine the night of the Harvest Moon dance

—the gazebo we'd decorated together lit by lanterns, music drifting across the village green, Asher asking me to dance in the space we'd created.

## Chapter Six

### ASHER

I stood outside Enchanted Threads with art supplies I hadn't touched in three years. The wooden box felt wrong in my hands. Too light for what it carried, too heavy for what it was. Through the shop window, Quinn arranged vintage hats on a display. She glanced up, caught me hesitating on the sidewalk, and her smile could have powered the whole street. She reached the door before I could reconsider.

"You came." She sounded breathless, like she'd been worried I wouldn't show.

"Said I would." I lifted the box slightly. "I brought art supplies. Not sure anything in here still works."

"Only one way to find out." She stepped back, holding the door wide. "Come on. I've got the space all set up."

The shop smelled like old fabric and lavender. She led me through racks of costumes—a Victorian gown with actual petticoats, flapper dresses with beaded fringe, what looked like a surprisingly accurate suit of armor—to a door at the back I hadn't noticed before.

"Here." She pushed it open, and afternoon light poured through.

The back room was smaller than I'd expected but the windows were massive—south and west facing, flooding everything with October gold. She'd cleared the space completely except for an old wooden easel, a small table, and a worn armchair pushed into the corner. Through the back window, I could see the edge of the village green where our gazebo stood, the café's roofline, the church steeple rising above the trees.

"I know it's not much," Quinn said, fidgeting with her sweater hem. "But the light's good in the afternoons, and it's quiet, and you can leave supplies here if you want. I never use this space anyway."

"It's perfect. Thank you."

"Don't thank me yet. You haven't tried to paint anything." She moved to the windows, adjusting the curtains. "Do you need anything? Water? Coffee? I could leave you alone if that's better, or I could stay if you want company while you set up, or—"

"Quinn."

She stopped, turning to face me.

"You're nervous," I said.

"Little bit." She wrapped her arms around herself. "I just want this to be good for you. Want you to remember why you did it before you stopped."

Something warm expanded behind my ribs. "Stay. If you want. While I set up."

Her smile made every bit of vulnerability worth it.

I set the box on the table and opened it slowly, like the contents might judge me for the years of neglect. Everything was still there—brushes with bristles gone stiff, paint tubes that might be completely dried out, palette knives I'd collected over years of learning my craft. My hands trembled as I lifted out the first brush.

"These are beautiful," Quinn said, picking up one of my palette knives carefully. "This must have been expensive."

"A gift from my mom before she died." The words came out before I could stop them. "She always believed I'd be an artist. Even when everyone else thought I should do something practical."

"She was right." Quinn set the knife down gently. "What would you paint? If you could paint anything right now?"

I looked at the empty canvas on the easel, at the afternoon light streaming through the windows, at Quinn watching me with complete faith that I could create something worth seeing.

"I don't know," I admitted. "It's been a while. I'm not sure I remember how."

"Your hands remember. Trust them." She settled into the armchair, curling her legs under her. "I'll just sit here quietly. Pretend I'm not here."

"You're hard to ignore."

"I'm choosing to take that as a compliment." Her voice was soft, encouraging. "Paint, Asher. Stop thinking and just paint."

I squeezed paint onto the palette—titanium white, burnt umber, cadmium yellow. Some tubes resisted, dried around the caps, but enough came through. The smell of linseed oil hit me, and for a moment I couldn't breathe. That smell was wrapped in a barrage of memories. Canvases I'd abandoned, dreams I'd packed away, the version of myself I'd decided wasn't practical enough to keep.

My hand shook as I picked up my favorite brush, the one Mom had spent too much money on. The handle felt foreign against my palm, like meeting an old friend who'd become a stranger.

I loaded the brush with paint. Lifted it to the canvas.

And froze.

The bristles hovered an inch from the surface, my entire arm locked. What if I'd forgotten? What if the years had erased whatever skill I'd built? What if the brush touched canvas and nothing happened, or worse, something terrible happened, and I'd have proof that I'd been right to give this up?

"Asher?" Quinn's voice was gentle. "You okay?"

"Yeah." I forced the word out. "Just... thinking."

"Stop thinking," she said again. "Just one stroke. See what happens."

I pressed the brush to canvas.

The first stroke was wrong. Too heavy, too uncertain, the color muddy where it should have been clear. My stomach dropped. See? This was why I'd stopped. Why I'd chosen handiwork, chosen practical, chosen safe.

I nearly set the brush down. Nearly said thank you anyway and left before I could prove to Quinn that she'd been wrong about me.

But my hand moved again. A second stroke, lighter this time. Then a third. The color spread, and muscle memory whispered instructions my conscious mind had forgotten. Load brush. Apply paint. Step back. Assess. Move forward.

The rhythm came back slowly, like remembering how to breathe after being underwater for too long. My hand steadied. The painting started making decisions for me—where the next color should go, how the light should fall, which details mattered and which were just noise.

Time disappeared.

I was distantly aware of Quinn in the armchair, perfectly still, like she'd sensed the importance of this moment and was afraid to break my concentration. But mostly I was just lost in the work, in the meditation of color and light and the physical act of creating something from nothing.

The painting emerged gradually. Not the village green as it actually looked, but as it felt—the gazebo glowing like it held magic, autumn light falling in gold sheets, shadows suggesting rather than defining. The trees weren't precise, the buildings weren't accurate, but the emotion was right. The sense of belonging. Of home.

At some point—an hour in, maybe more—my hand cramped and I had to stop. I stepped back, shaking out my fingers, and caught Quinn watching me.

Not the painting. Me.

Her expression stopped my breath. Wonder mixed with something softer, something that made my chest feel too tight and too full at the same time. Like she was seeing me, truly seeing me, not the man I'd become but the artist I'd abandoned.

Our gazes met. She didn't look away.

"Asher." Her voice was barely above a whisper. "That's extraordinary."

I turned back to the canvas, trying to see what she saw. The village green at sunset. Our gazebo. But transformed into something that existed between memory and reality and dream. Not photorealistic exactly. No, it was more impressionistic. More emotional. Sort of like how I used to paint before my mom died.

"It's rough. Needs a lot of work," I managed to say.

"It's perfect." She uncurled from the chair and moved closer, stopping just behind my shoulder. Close enough that warmth radiated from her. "The way you captured the light—it doesn't just look like the green. It feels like yesterday."

My throat constricted. "That's what I was trying to find. Didn't know it until I painted it."

"This is who you are." She was still staring at the canvas, her voice full of certainty. "Not despite the handiwork, but alongside it. You're allowed to be both, Asher. Creative and helpful."

"Maybe," I muttered, sighing. "Do you have a sink where I can clean up?"

She didn't look particularly pleased with my *maybe*, but she didn't argue. Instead, she showed me to a small bathroom and I went to work cleaning the brushes, making sure not to leave any globs or streaks of paint anywhere. I finished cleaning the brushes, organizing everything. When I returned to the room, the painting sat on the easel, wet and unfinished, and Quinn was staring at it again.

"It really is beautiful," she said, glancing at me when I lingered in the doorway. The sun kissed the side of her face, turning her auburn hair into a halo of fire around her. If anything was beautiful, it was her, and I had a sudden urge to tear up the canvas I'd painted and start again with a better subject to create. I didn't realize I'd been staring until she said my name.

"What?" I cleared my throat, and put the box of supplies on the table.

"I said that you could probably sell this on Etsy or something."

"Nah, too complicated."

"It's not that complicated. I've sold a couple costume pieces on there. I could show you sometime if you change your mind." She crossed the room and checked her phone, frowning. "You know what's strange?" Quinn unplugged her phone from the outlet near the table. "This is the third time today it's died. I think the battery's going."

"Could be the outlet." I noticed a faint scorch mark on the wall plate. "This building's pretty old. When's the last time you had the wiring checked?"

"Um." She bit her lip. "Never? I inherited the shop as-is from the previous owner."

"You should get it looked at. Old wiring can be dangerous." I pointed at the outlet. "See that mark? That's not great."

"I'll add it to the list." She wound the charging cable around her phone. "Right after costume finishing and booth prep and approximately seventeen other things."

"Quinn."

"I know, I know. I'll call someone." But her tone suggested she was already mentally deprioritizing it, and I made a note to remind her later.

"I should go," I said, instead of everything else I wanted to say. "Let you get back to work."

"You could stay longer. Paint more. I don't close until six."

"I'm supposed to help Sawyer unpack some stuff. He's got a lot going on with Maple and his ex." I dried my hands on my jeans, buying time. "But I'll come back. If that's okay."

"More than okay. Tomorrow?" She sounded hopeful. "Or is that too soon? I don't want to push, I just—"

"Tomorrow works." I finally made myself meet her eyes, and the smile that lit her face made my ribs feel too tight. "Same time?"

"Perfect."

She walked me to the front door, and we stood in that awkward space between goodbye and not wanting to leave.

"Asher?" She touched my arm lightly. "Thank you for trusting me with this. I know it wasn't easy."

"You made it easier. Not because you made me want to paint. Just... being with you reminds me who I was before my mom passed."

Her eyes went soft. "I'm glad. And for the record? I like who you are now. The handyman who paints. Both versions at once."

I left before I could say something cringy.

At home, I pulled out a smaller canvas I'd found—not for anything specific, just to have ready. Just in case tomorrow turned into a habit.

My phone buzzed.

> Thank you for today. The painting is beautiful. You're beautiful. I mean your ART is beautiful. Obviously. I'm going to stop texting now before I say something else embarrassing.

I read it three times, my mouth curving despite everything.

Your embarrassing texts are kind of endearing.

That's a relief because I have a lot of them.

See you tomorrow.

Can't wait.

# Chapter Seven

## QUINN

"Absolutely not." Asher stared at the Victorian gentleman's costume like I'd just asked him to wear his niece's tutu.

"Come on." I held up the burgundy jacket with its brass buttons and velvet lapels. The fabric caught the afternoon light streaming through my shop windows. "I need to see how it looks on someone who's not a mannequin. You're the perfect size."

"Find another perfect size."

"You're already here. And it would be fun," I said, waggling my eyebrows

"That's not—" He stopped, jaw tightening. "Your definition of fun is very different from mine." He ran a hand through his hair and sighed. "But... fine. One costume."

"Three minimum."

"One."

"Four, and I won't make you wear the giant pumpkin suit."

His eyes narrowed. "There's a giant pumpkin suit?"

"With a stem hat."

"Three costumes. Final offer."

I grinned, already pulling the pirate outfit from the rack. "Deal. Changing room's all yours."

He took the Victorian jacket and headed toward the back, muttering something I didn't quite catch. I arranged the other costumes on the counter, mentally cataloging what still needed hemming before the festival.

"Okay." Asher's voice carried from the back. "This is happening."

He stepped out, and I dropped the spool of thread I was holding.

The Victorian jacket fit him perfectly, emphasizing his shoulders in a way that made my brain temporarily forget how to function. The high collar framed his jaw, and the whole effect was so unexpectedly attractive that I had to remind myself to breathe.

"You're staring." He tugged at the collar, ears going pink.

"You look—" I bent to pick up the thread, buying myself time to form coherent thoughts. "The proportions are perfect."

"I feel ridiculous."

"You look like you stepped out of a Jane Austen novel." I circled him slowly, pretending to examine the fit while absolutely noticing how good he looked. "Though the collar needs adjusting."

I reached up to fix it, my fingers brushing the warm skin of his neck, and he went very still. His pulse jumped under my touch.

"Quinn."

"Hmm?" I was focused on the fabric, on getting the angle right, on definitely not thinking about how close we were standing.

"You're enjoying this."

"Oh definitely." I stepped back, satisfied with the collar even though I could've adjusted it from arm's length. "Next one."

The pirate outfit came with a tricorn hat that Asher refused to touch.

"No."

"It's part of the costume."

"I'm wearing the shirt and jacket. The hat stays off."

"That defeats the entire pirate aesthetic." I picked up the hat, holding it out. "Just try it. It's not like I'm making you wear an eye patch and a hook."

"Quinn—"

"Are you scared of a hat?"

His mouth flattened. "Of course not."

"Then put it on."

We stared at each other for a long moment, and I could see the exact second he realized I wasn't backing down. He reached for the hat, but I pulled it back.

"Nope. I'll do it." I stepped close, rising on my toes to settle the hat on his head. It sat at an angle, slightly rakish, and combined with the open collar of the white shirt, he looked like he was about to sail off to plunder something.

"There." My hands were still raised, adjusting the angle, and I was very aware of the space between us shrinking. "Perfect."

"I look like I'm going to a costume party."

"Well, this is a costume shop. What did you expect? And you look like you could rescue someone from a cursed ship."

"That's worse." But his mouth curved upwards.

The 1920s gangster suit was when I lost the ability to pretend this was supposed to be productive.

He stepped out of the back room, and I actually had to turn away and pretend to organize thread. The pinstripes, the vest, the way the whole outfit somehow made him look dangerous. It was doing things to my heart rate.

"That bad?" he asked, and there was something in his voice that made me look up.

He knew. He could see exactly what effect he was having, and he wasn't making it easier for me.

"You should dress like this all the time," I managed.

"I don't think the suit would fare well while I'm digging around in crawlspaces or fixing roofs."

"Maybe, but you look like you own a speakeasy." I moved closer because apparently I'd lost all sense of self-preservation. "This one's my favorite."

"Yeah?" His voice dropped lower. "Good to know."

He disappeared into the back again, and I was a little bummed that he was going to change. Okay, a lot bummed. Not that he wasn't handsome in his normal clothes, but the man could pull off a fedora.

"Uh, Quinn... I think I'm stuck." His voice came from the changing room.

My eyebrows shot up. "Stuck how?"

"The vest. The buttons won't—just come here."

I bit my lip, took a steadying breath that did nothing at all, and went to the changing room. I knocked twice, and he opened the door. He was struggling with the tiny vest buttons. His hair was messed up from pulling shirts on and off, and there was something endearing about his frustration.

"These buttons hate me specifically," he said.

I laughed, stepping close to work the stubborn buttons free. "They're just old. Here, let me." I was a little too aware of his chest rising and falling under my hands, of the paint stains still on his fingers from yesterdays work in my back room.

"There." I freed the last button, but neither of us stepped back.

"Quinn—"

My phone alarm went off. The hayride. We had forty minutes to get to his brother's farm where the rest of the town and a whole host of tourists would be waiting.

"We should go," I said, stepping back too quickly. "I'll just—I need to change."

"Right. Yeah." He looked down at the costume. "I should probably not wear this."

By the time we reached the start of the hayride, the sun was starting its descent toward the horizon and families were gathering around the wagon. Levi stood by the tractor, and Amberlyn, the woman who'd enjoyed my ideas at the town meeting, had a clipboard.

"Quinn! Asher!" She waved us over. "Are you both riding? There's plenty of room."

We climbed onto the flatbed wagon lined with hay bales. The air had that October bite that made me glad I'd worn my jacket. Asher settled beside me, and when I shivered, he shifted closer without a word, his shoulder against mine.

I didn't see Sawyer and Maple around, but people were still arriving. From what Asher told me, most of the first round of riders would be local, and then the tourists would start arriving later.

The tractor rumbled to life, and we lurched forward into the

October evening. I glanced at Asher and smirked. "Mayor Goldwin's going to be insufferable when he hears about this. Your aunt too."

"Hears about what?" His mouth curved.

"Us. Together. On the hayride." I settled more comfortably against his side, his warmth seeping through my jacket. "The mayor isn't subtle about his meddling."

"Definitely not."

Amberlyn's voice carried back to us, telling stories about the founding families and the agricultural heritage of Acorn Field Heights.

"Can I ask you something?" I said after a while.

"Sure."

"Why did you really agree to help me with the festival? You didn't really know me."

He was quiet for a moment, his hand tapping a rhythm on his knee. "Mayor Goldwin has a way of making you feel guilty if you say no. And maybe I was curious."

"About the festival?"

"About you." His voice was low enough that only I could hear it. "New person in town, actually excited about Acorn Field Heights. It was different."

"Different good or different weird?"

"Maybe a bit of both." He winked at me.

By the time we returned, stars had appeared and I was shivering despite Asher's warmth. He helped me down from the wagon, his hands steady on my waist, and we headed to a few of the booths.

The conversation was easy, and on more than one occasion, he made me laugh. I didn't realize how late it had gotten until I started yawning.

"Can I walk you to your car?" he offered.

"Sure."

We were halfway to the cars when I saw him.

Carter stood near the entrance to the festival grounds, hands in the pockets of his expensive wool coat, looking completely out of place among the families in flannel and fleece. He was scanning the crowd, and when his gaze landed on me, his expression shifted into something that looked like relief mixed with determination.

My feet stopped moving.

"Quinn?" Asher's hand was still on my elbow from helping me navigate around a hay bale. "What's wrong?"

But I couldn't answer because Carter was already walking toward us, his confident stride eating up the distance. He looked exactly the same as he had when I'd left—perfectly styled hair, designer jeans, that smile that used to make me feel special and now just made my stomach clench.

"There you are." He reached us, and before I could react, he pulled me into a hug. I went stiff in his arms, my hands awkwardly trapped between us. "I've been looking everywhere for you. I texted, but you didn't respond."

"Carter." I stepped back as soon as he released me, my heart hammering against my ribs. "What are you doing here? You said—"

"I know, I know. But I couldn't wait." His attention flicked to Asher, then back to me, and something calculating crossed his face. "We need to talk, Quinn. It's important."

"Carter, this is Asher." My voice came out smaller than I wanted it to. I cleared my throat, trying to find the confidence I'd felt just moments ago. "We're working on the festival together."

"Right. The festival." Carter's tone suggested he thought the entire concept was quaint and slightly ridiculous. He extended his hand to Asher. "Carter Reynolds. Quinn's boyfriend."

"Ex-boyfriend," I corrected, but my voice was still too quiet.

"We should talk about that." Carter's hand landed on my shoulder. "That's why I'm here."

Asher's jaw tightened, and his gaze flicked from Carter to me and back again. When his eyes met mine, I wanted to say something, to explain, to tell him this wasn't what I wanted. But the words stuck in my throat.

"Quinn and I were just leaving," Asher said, his voice carefully neutral.

"Perfect. I'll walk with you." Carter's hand stayed on my shoulder. "We have a lot to catch up on."

I should have said no.

"Okay."

The word came out automatically.

Asher's expression shuttered. "I'll see you tomorrow then. For the festival prep."

"Asher—" I started, but I didn't know what to say. My thoughts were tangled, my confidence from earlier in the evening evaporating like it had never existed.

"It's fine." But his voice said it wasn't fine, not at all. "Night, Quinn."

He walked away, hands shoved in his pockets, and I watched him go with a sinking feeling in my chest. This was wrong. I knew it was wrong. But Carter was already steering me toward the parking lot, talking about his drive and how surprised I'd be when I heard his news, and I was letting him, falling back into old patterns.

"I can't believe you've been hiding out here. It's charming, I guess. Very small town. But Quinn, we need to talk about your future. Our future."

"I'm not hiding." The words came out defensive, and I hated how he'd put me on the back foot within minutes. "I live here now."

"Right. That's what we need to discuss. I have some opportunities that I think you'll be excited about. Things that make more sense than running a costume shop in the middle of nowhere."

We reached my car, and I fumbled with my keys, my hands shaking. The evening that had felt so perfect an hour ago now felt distant, like something I'd imagined. Asher's knee bumping me on the hayride, the way he'd looked at me in the moonlight, the growing certainty that I was building something real here—all of it felt fragile now, like it might shatter if Carter kept talking.

"I should go," I managed. "It's late, and I have a lot to do tomorrow."

"Of course. Where are you staying? I got a room at some bed and breakfast." He pulled out his phone. "Let me text you the address. We can have breakfast tomorrow and really talk."

"I don't know if I'm free—"

"Make time, Quinn." His voice was gentle, but there was steel underneath it. "This is important. I drove all this way to see you."

"Okay," I heard myself say again. I hated that word. That automatic, conflict-avoiding, people-pleasing word.

Carter smiled, satisfied, and kissed my forehead before I could move away. "That's my girl. I'll text you in the morning. Get some rest. We have a lot to figure out."

He walked away, leaving me standing next to my car in the October cold.

I sat in my car for a long time before starting the engine, staring at the booths where families were still wandering, where Asher had probably already driven home, where an hour ago I'd felt happy and hopeful and like I was exactly where I was supposed to be.

My phone buzzed with a text from Carter. Then another. Plans for tomorrow. Each message was a small claim on my time, my attention, my life.

I drove home in a daze, changed into pajamas mechanically, climbed into bed without my usual routine.

Outside my window, Acorn Field Heights was quiet under its blanket of stars. Asher was probably wondering what had just happened. Probably regretting the whole afternoon. And I didn't know how to fix it.

# Chapter Eight

## ASHER

Quinn's ex-boyfriend was in her shop holding two coffee cups and grinning at her like he owned the place.

I stopped in the doorway, my own gas station thermos suddenly feeling cheap in my hand. Carter wore and expensive coat, stood with confident posture, and had the kind of smile that probably worked on everyone. Everyone but me, it would seem, because I flat out refused to return that smile.

"Asher, right?" He shifted both cups to one hand and extended the other. "Carter Reynolds."

"We also met last night," I muttered, shaking his hand because refusing would make me look petty. He had a firm grip. I looked past him to where Quinn stood behind the register, watching us. "Didn't realize you were coming to town this early."

"Change of plans." He turned to Quinn. "Figured why wait?"

"You weren't supposed to arrive until the twenty-third," Quinn said, taking one of the coffee cups he offered. The logo was from that expensive place two towns over, the kind with actual latte art. "I told you—"

"I know what you said, but I was worried about you." His tone was gentle, reasonable. "An eight hour drive isn't that far when someone you care about needs support."

The word "support" didn't give me a warm and fuzzy feeling, and by the look of it, Quinn had a similar reaction. I set my thermos on the counter, aware of how shabby it looked next to his polished cups. Quinn's eyes flicked to it, then to me, something apologetic crossing her face.

"Well." I picked up a box of decorations I'd left yesterday. "I should get these to the green. Mayor Goldwin wanted the gazebo decorations for the dance adjusted."

"Wait, I thought we were working on the costume booth first?" Quinn moved around the counter. "I have some fabric samples I wanted you to see—"

"You two go ahead. I'll catch up later." I was already backing toward the door, needing air, needing distance from whatever this was. Behind me, I heard Carter say something about the shop being "charming, in a small-town way," and Quinn's polite laugh scraped against my ribs.

Outside, October morning light turned the village green amber and gold. Through the shop window, I watched Carter lean against Quinn's counter, completely at ease in her space. He said something that made her tilt her head, listening in a focused way. They looked like people who knew each other's rhythms, who had history and inside jokes and all the things I didn't.

I forced myself to walk to the gazebo and not look back.

The rest of Sunday passed in fragments of Carter being there. At the gazebo, standing close while they looked at her phone. By the sidewalk, touching her arm to get her attention. Near steps of the café, his hand briefly on her lower back as he guided her past a hay bale.

Nothing threatening. Just comfortable. Familiar. The casual touches of someone who'd done it a thousand times before.

I worked. Adjusted hay bales. Secured loose decorations. Hammered stakes deeper than necessary into ground that didn't need it.

"You're going to hit bedrock," Levi said around four, appearing with a box of supplies and that older-brother expression I had the sudden urge to remove from his face with my fist.

"Just making sure it's secure."

"You're making sure you don't have to look at them." He set down the box. "Who is the new guy?"

"Her ex."

Levi was quiet for a moment, watching Quinn and Carter across the green. They were examining a banner, their heads bent together. "You know what's worse than wanting something you can't have?"

"What?"

"Giving up before you know for sure you can't have it." He squeezed my shoulder. "Don't be like me, Ash. Don't wait eight years to figure out what matters."

He walked away before I could respond, leaving me with a hammer and the uncomfortable knowledge that my brother was right. Except Levi hadn't seen the way Carter looked at Quinn, hadn't seen the way she looked back.

By the time I got home Sunday evening, Sawyer had already heard—probably from Aunt Caroline, who saw everything and told everyone.

"So," he said, finding me in the barn where I was helping Levi reorganize some tools. "Quinn's ex is back."

"News travels fast."

"It's Acorn Field Heights. News travels before it happens." He leaned against the workbench. "How are you doing?"

"Fine."

"Liar."

I set down the wrench I'd been holding. "What do you want me to say, Sawyer? That it sucks watching Quinn with her ex? That I'm the guy with dirt under his fingernails while Carter's the guy who can actually help her?"

"There it is." He crossed his arms. "You have feelings for her."

"Obviously."

"So what are you going to do about it?"

I laughed, but there was no humor in it. "What can I do? Carter can solve her money problems, and I'm offering what—half-planned sketches and festival decorations?"

"You're offering yourself. Which is worth more than you think." Sawyer's voice carried the same tone he used on his daughter to get through to her that she had made a mistake. "But if you're going to stand here feeling sorry for yourself instead of fighting for what you want, then yeah—this Carter guy has already won."

"Uncle Asher!" Maple appeared in the barn doorway wearing her favorite purple tutu. "Why are you hiding?"

"I'm not hiding, kiddo. Just working."

She studied me with those too-observant eyes. "You look sad. Like when Daddy talked about Mommy leaving. Is it because of the pretty costume lady?"

Sawyer lifted her onto his hip. "Inside thoughts, remember?"

"But it's true." She looked between us. "He gets all smiley when she's around, and now he's not smiley anymore."

"Out of the mouths of babes," Sawyer muttered. To me, he said, "Don't give up yet. Sometimes things aren't what they look like."

But time proved things were exactly what they looked like.

I saw them at the hardware store mid-morning, Carter holding paint samples while Quinn nodded at something he was saying. I ducked down the plumbing aisle before they could see me, then left through the back exit like a coward.

My phone buzzed as I reached my truck.

> Hey! Thought I saw you at the hardware store? Did you leave?

I stared at the text, then typed back.

> Yeah, had to get back to worksite. Talk later.

> Okay. Miss working with you.

I shoved my phone in my pocket and drove away.
The next day, she texted again.

> Coffee? Want to show you the final booth sketches.

I waited an hour before responding.

Busy today. Looks great in the photos though.

You sure? I could bring coffee to you.

Rain check?

The dots appeared and disappeared several times before her final message came through.

Okay. Let me know when you have time.

I didn't respond.

The next morning, we were supposed to meet about booth setup. I texted at seven.

Something came up. Can you handle it?

Her response was immediate.

Of course. Everything okay?

Fine. Just busy.

Asher, are you avoiding me?

The question sat on my screen, deserving an honest answer I couldn't give.

No. Just a lot going on.

Are you still coming to the dance?

Not sure.

Honestly, I didn't want to see her dancing with him. I was jealous. I could admit it. Just not to her.

I watched those three dots appear and disappear for five full minutes before she finally responded.

Okay.

That single word carried more weight than anything else she could have written.

Finally, I broke down and drove to the village green, telling myself I needed to check the decorations for the dance. Not that I was hoping to see her. Not that the distance between us was making it hard to breathe.

I found her alone, hanging garlands. Relief crossed her face when she saw me.

"Asher." She climbed down from the stepladder. "I was starting to think you'd disappeared."

"Just been busy." The lie tasted worse each time I told it.

"Right. Busy." She wrapped her arms around herself, and October wind caught her hair. She was wearing a blue scarf that looked expensive. "Can we talk? I feel like something's wrong, and I don't understand what happened."

"Nothing happened."

"That's not true. Ever since the hayride, you've been distant. You barely respond to my texts, you canceled our meeting, and you're looking at me right now like I'm a stranger." Her voice cracked slightly. "Did I do something wrong?"

*Yes. No. You let Carter back into your life when I was stupid enough to think we had something. You're wearing what is likely a scarf from him and drinking his fancy coffee and considering his offers when I have nothing to offer you but dirt under my fingernails and a third-place pumpkin carving ribbon.*

"You didn't do anything wrong." I shoved my hands in my pockets. "I just think maybe you should consider what Carter's offering."

She blinked. "What?"

"He drove hours to help you. He can solve your money problems, help with your shop. That's worth considering."

"Are you serious right now?" Her voice went sharp. "You're telling me to get back together with my ex?"

"I'm telling you to be practical. He can give you security. Stability. Things you need." *Things I can't give you.*

"I can't believe this." She laughed, but there was no humor in it. "Three days ago, we were working together every day. And now you're pushing me toward Carter?"

"I'm trying to help you make a smart choice."

"By avoiding me? By canceling our meetings and barely responding to my texts?" She stepped closer, and I could see the hurt in her eyes. "If you don't want to be around me, just say so. Don't pretend you're being noble."

I wasn't being noble—I was being a coward. Too scared to watch her choose Carter, too scared to fight for something I'd probably lose anyway.

"I'm not pretending anything." My jaw was so tight it hurt. "I'm being realistic. Carter can help you in ways I can't."

"I don't want Carter's help. I want—" She stopped, shook her head. "You know what? Forget it. If this is how you handle things when they get complicated, then maybe distance is better."

She walked away before I could respond, leaving me standing in the October afternoon with the taste of failure in my mouth.

I drove home and found Sawyer in my kitchen, making dinner while Maple colored in a coloring book.

"I already regret giving you a key," I muttered, tossing my jacket on a chair.

"Went well then, did it?" he asked, taking one look at my face.

"About as well as expected."

"Which means you pushed her away instead of fighting for her."

I slumped into a chair, watching Maple color. "I told her to consider Carter's offer. He can actually help her keep the shop open."

"And you can't?"

"Not like he can. I'm a handyman, Sawyer. Carter has money, stability, everything she needs." I rubbed my face. "I'm trying to do the right thing."

"The right thing," Sawyer said slowly, as if I were the same age as his daughter, "would be telling her how you feel. The coward's thing is pushing her toward someone else because you're too scared to risk getting hurt."

"It's not about being scared—"

"It's exactly about being scared." He set down the spoon he'd been using. "You're terrified she'll choose him, so you're making the choice for her. You're deciding you're not good enough without giving her a chance to decide for herself. You're going to the dance, right?"

I shrugged. "I was going to, but—"

"But now you're being a little baby?"

"Uncle Asher's not a baby," Maple said with a frown.

"Thanks kid," I said, flashing her a grin before glaring at my brother. "I'm not being a baby. I'm being reasonable. Besides, I'm not a glutton for punishment, and that's exactly what watching her with him at the dance will be."

"Stop deciding what's best for her and let her make her own choices. Even if she chooses Carter—which she might—at least you'll know you fought for it.

"What if I already ruined it?" I mumbled.

"Then you apologize and try to fix it." Sawyer returned to stirring whatever was in the pot. "But do it before the dance and she decides you're not worth the trouble."

That night, I lay in bed staring at the ceiling, Sawyer's words circling in my head. My phone sat on the nightstand, Quinn's unanswered texts glowing in the dark.

I should call her. Apologize. Explain that I was scared and stupid and sorry. Tell her that watching Carter touch her arm and bring her fancy coffee made me feel about two inches tall, but that wasn't her fault or her problem to fix.

Instead, I rolled over and tried to sleep, convincing myself that maybe tomorrow I'd find the courage to tell her everything. That I'd stop being noble or cowardly or whatever this was and just be honest.

Tomorrow. I'd fix it tomorrow at the dance.

# Chapter Nine

## QUINN

It was far too late for Carter to be sitting across from me at my worktable, the same spot where Asher and I sketched ideas. I was already tired and emotional, and for the life of me, I could not stop yawning.

"I want to help you, Quinn." Carter pulled out his phone, tapped the screen a few times, then turned it toward me. "I've put together some numbers."

A spreadsheet. Of course he'd made a spreadsheet.

"Shop repairs first." He scrolled down with his thumb. "Window replacement, roof leak, electrical issues. I've already talked to contractors. That's eight thousand, give or take."

The number sat there on his screen. My credit cards were maxed out at twelve thousand. The contractors had given me estimates three weeks ago that I'd filed in my mental drawer labeled "Problems For Future Quinn."

Future Quinn probably hated me with a burning passion at this point...

"Your credit cards." Another scroll. "I can pay those off. Clean slate. You'd be debt-free for the first time since you opened this place."

Debt-free. I wondered what that was like.

"There's also a position at my company." He set the phone down between us. "Marketing coordinator. It's exactly what you're good at—visual presentation, brand storytelling, customer experience. The salary is fifty-five thousand, full benefits package, health insurance, dental, 401k matching. You can sell the shop and come back to the city with me after the festival. Leave all this stress behind."

My ribs tightened. "Carter—"

"I know what you're thinking." He leaned forward, his hands open on the table like he had nothing to hide. "You think I'm trying to control you. Make your decisions for you. But I'm not, I swear. I'm just laying out options. Unfortunately, you don't have many. But, you don't have to decide right now."

Options. He was giving me options. That's what people did when they cared about you, wasn't it? They helped. They offered solutions instead of watching you drown.

"Just think about it." He reached across the table and squeezed my hand. "Look at yourself, Quinn. You're exhausted. You've lost weight. When's the last time you slept through the night?" His thumb traced across my knuckles. "This place is killing you. I can see it. Everyone can see it."

Was it? Or was I just tired? There had to be a difference, except right now I couldn't remember what it was.

"I need to think about it," I managed.

"That's all I'm asking." He stood, buttoning his coat. "I've got a meeting tomorrow night, but I'll speak to you the next day. And Quinn, this is a great opportunity. Maybe don't think too long." He paused at the door. "I care about you. I always have. Just let me help you."

After he left, I sat in the quiet shop surrounded by costumes I'd carefully curated and debts I couldn't pay, and tried to remember why I'd thought opening this place was a good idea.

The morning crawled by in slow motion. I helped Mrs. Oakley find a flapper dress for her granddaughter, restocked the Renaissance section, checked the festival booth inventory for the third time this week. Normal tasks that felt surreal, like I was watching someone else's hands move through the motions.

Around eleven, I saw Asher across the village green through my front window. He was unloading hay bales from his truck, his shoulders flexing under his flannel shirt as he lifted each one. Aunt Caroline stood nearyby and said something that made him laugh, his whole face transforming.

I lifted my hand to wave.

He glanced toward my shop. Our eyes met for half a second. Then he turned back like I'd been dismissed.

The casual rejection lodged somewhere under my sternum.

I pulled out my phone and took several seconds trying to figure out what to type.

> Did the mayor approve the dance decorations?

The three dots appeared almost immediately, and his response came through.

> Yeah, he said it looks good

I stared at the words, then typed out two words.

> Coffee later?

The dots took longer this time.

> Sorry. Got a lot of prep to do before the dance

I set my phone face-down on the counter and went back to rearranging displays. When I looked back, he was gone, which I tried to convince myself was a good thing.

Much to my dismay, the Harvest Moon Dance started at seven, and by six forty-five I was standing in front of my closet trying to convince myself not to go.

Carter had texted twice already about his meeting, adding that he'd stop by the shop tomorrow to "check in." The relief I felt at his absence made me feel guilty, which made me feel worse about everything else.

I pulled on a navy sweater dress and boots, did something with my hair that was supposed to look effortless but took twenty minutes, and walked to the village green before I could change my mind.

The parking on the streets was already full. People were dancing, talking, laughing. Paper lanterns I'd made hung from the ceiling of the gazebo, casting warm light across the moving bodies.

I took a breath and joined the fray.

The music was upbeat, some folksy tune with fiddles that had couples spinning across the makeshift dance floor. I spotted Mayor Goldwin near the refreshment table, Aunt Caroline chatting with the town gossip, Dolores, by the edge of the gazebo, and families clustered in groups around the edges of the dance floor.

When Dolores left Aunt Caroline alone, I made my way over, weaving through dancers and trying not to look like I was searching for someone specific, even though I absolutely was.

"Quinn!" Aunt Caroline's face lit up when she saw me. "You made it! And those lanterns—they're absolutely perfect. The whole place looks magical."

"Thank you. I'm glad they turned out okay." I glanced around, trying to be casual. "Is Asher here?"

Something shifted in Caroline's expression. "I haven't seen him yet. But knowing my nephew, he's probably still at work fussing over something that doesn't need fussing over." She squeezed my arm. "I'm sure he'll show up eventually."

Eventually. Right.

I thanked her and drifted toward the refreshment table, accepting a cup of cider I didn't want and positioning myself where I could watch for a specific tall man without being obvious about it. Maple ran past with two other children, laughing as they wove between adults. I caught sight of Levi talking to Amberlyn near the DJ booth, and Sawyer was on the dance floor with Isla, both of them looking happy and comfortable together.

Everyone seemed to be having a good time.

I checked my phone. Seven thirty. No messages.

Maybe he wasn't coming. Maybe he'd decided that whatever was starting between us wasn't worth the complication of my ex showing up and me turning back into someone he didn't recognize. Someone who said "okay" when she meant "no," who let other people make her decisions, who couldn't even send a text without overthinking it.

I set down my untouched cider. This was a mistake. I should go home, get some sleep, figure out what I was going to tell Carter tomorrow.

"The decorations really are perfect."

I spun around.

Asher stood a few feet away, hands in his pockets, looking uncomfortable. He wore a dark green button-down shirt I'd never seen before, and his hair looked like he'd attempted to tame it with mixed results.

"You're here." The words came out more accusatory than I'd intended.

"I'm as surprised as you are." He took a step closer. "Can we talk?"

"Sure. Yes. Absolutely." I was already moving toward the street, desperate to get out of the crowded area where people were starting to notice us standing together. "Wanna go for a walk?"

The music faded as we left the dance behind us. The air was cold enough to make me pull my jacket tighter, and above us the stars were sharp and clear against the dark sky.

We started walking without discussing direction, falling into step beside each other on the sidewalk. For a block, neither of us spoke. The crunch of our footsteps, the distant sound of the dance, the hammering of my own heart were all louder than the lack of conversation.

"I'm sorry," we both said at the same time.

We stopped walking. Looked at each other.

"You don't have anything to apologize for," Asher said.

"Yes I do. I've been—" I gestured helplessly. "Carter showed up and I just... I panicked. I became this person I didn't want to be anymore, and I know he means well, but he just sort of takes over and I said 'okay' when I meant 'absolutely not,' and I've been a mess since he got here, and you've been avoiding me—"

"I wasn't avoiding you," he interrupted, then stopped. "Okay, I was avoiding you. But not because of anything you did."

"Then why?"

He ran a hand through his hair, messing up whatever order he'd managed. "Because I watched you with him, and I saw how familiar you two were. I know he's capable and has money and his life together. And I questioned what I had to offer you." He looked at me, his face unguarded for the first time in a while. "I was giving you space to figure out what you wanted. Whether that was him or..."

"It's not him." The words burst out of me. "It's absolutely not him. I don't want Carter. I don't want to go back to the city. I don't want any of the things he thinks I should want."

"But?"

"But he's offering me solutions to all my problems." My voice cracked. "The shop repairs, my credit card debt, a job with actual benefits. He's laid it all out on a spreadsheet, and he's not wrong that I'm drowning here. And I hate that he's right about that part, even though everything else feels wrong."

We'd reached my shop without realizing it. The streetlight cast shadows across the front window where costumes hung on display, the space I'd poured everything into for the past few months.

"What do you want?" Asher murmured.

"I... I want to stay," I told the ground, shuffling my feet. "I want to keep building my own life here." I gestured at the shop, then at him, then at the town around us. "I want to make this work. I want to figure out how to pay my bills without selling my soul. I want to stop saying 'okay' to things that make me miserable." My throat tightened. "And I want to spend time with you."

"I'm sorry I made that difficult." Asher stepped closer. "I just...I didn't want to get in the way if you wanted something, or someone, else."

"And if I don't?"

His mouth curved upwards. "Then I'd like a second chance."

"Well," I said, shrugging. "I suppose this is the start of it." My gaze dropped to his mouth where he bit his lower lip. "What are you going to do about it?"

He glanced at my lips where I wore a smirk. "I have an idea."

"Oh yeah?"

We stood there on the sidewalk in front of my shop, close enough to see his breath fogging in the cold air, close enough that when I shifted my weight we were almost touching.

And then we *were* touching.

His hand rose up and cupped my face, his thumb brushing my cheekbone. He leaned down, and I rose up. Our mouths met somewhere in the middle.

The kiss was soft and careful and absolutely perfect. His other hand settled at my waist, drawing me closer, and I grabbed his shirt to keep my balance as the sidewalk seemed to tilt under my feet. He tasted like cider and autumn, and when we broke apart, my stomach was doing backflips.

"We should probably head back," I said, but I didn't move.

"Probably." He didn't either.

We stood there another moment, his forehead resting against mine, before he stepped back and offered his hand. I took it, lacing my fingers through his, and we started the walk back toward the village green. The music drifted through the streets, mingling with laughter and the rustle of corn stalks someone had tied to the streetlamps.

"Think anyone noticed we left?" I asked.

"In Acorn Field Heights?" He shot me a sideways look. "I'd put money on at least three people timing how long we were gone."

I laughed, the sound carrying in the cold air. "Fair point."

We walked back to the dance hand in hand, and when we stepped inside the gazebo, everything looked exactly the same as when I'd left.

Asher led me onto the dance floor as a slow song started, and I let him pull me close, my head resting against his shoulder. Around us, couples swayed and talked, and I caught Aunt Caroline's knowing smile from across the room. Mayor Goldwin looked positively smug.

"Everyone's staring," I murmured.

"Are they? I hadn't noticed." His hand was warm on my back, steady as he watched me with those careful eyes. "Just keep your eyes on me, and they'll all fade away."

He was right.

The song shifted into something slower, and Asher's thumb traced small circles against my spine. With Asher's arms around me and the autumn night wrapping us in its quiet chill, I felt like I was home.

# Chapter Ten

## QUINN

The burgundy velvet slid through my fingers, each stitch locking into place with the satisfying rhythm I'd come to crave. Eleven-thirty at night and I was still here, surrounded by half-finished costumes. A Renaissance gown draped across my worktable, all flowing sleeves and gold trim that caught the overhead light. Behind me, a pirate vest needed buttonholes, a flapper dress was missing fringe on one hip, and a Victorian mourning gown waited for its final jet beads.

My neck ached from hunching over the machine, but I didn't mind. Tomorrow was the Fall Festival. Tomorrow I'd have a booth on the village green where people could try on my costumes and take fun pictures with the gorgeous set Asher and I had designed.

I reached for my water bottle and found it empty. When had I last eaten? Lunch, maybe. Oh yeah, a turkey club sandwich Asher had brought me when he stopped by to fix my squeaky back door. He'd stayed for twenty minutes, asking questions about the mourning gown's construction while I explained Victorian beading techniques, and the whole time he'd looked at me like my answers actually mattered.

The bell above the door chimed.

My hand froze on the fabric. I'd forgotten to lock it.

"Sorry, we're closed," I called over the machine's hum. "But I open at nine tomorrow if—"

"Quinn."

The sewing machine's noise died as I hit the power switch. My pulse kicked up, rabbit-quick, and I turned to find Carter standing just inside the door. His wool coat was perfectly pressed, hands tucked in his pockets, face arranged in that carefully neutral expression I knew too well.

"Carter. Hi. What are you doing here so late?" I kept my voice level, but my fingers curled against the table's edge.

"Driving through. Saw your light." He took one step forward, dress shoes clicking against the hardwood. "Thought maybe we could talk. Just for a few minutes."

I stood, putting the worktable between us. The velvet gown pooled across the surface. "Talk about what?" I knew what he was going to say, but I foolishly had hoped he'd lost interest. I hadn't seen him since before the dance and had crossed my fingers that he'd gotten distracted and left. Wishful thinking, apparently.

"I know you needed time, but my deadline is tomorrow. I need an answer. So I'll ask one more time—are you coming back with me, or are you throwing away everything we worked for?"

"Carter, the offer was generous, but—"

"It was more than generous. Any smart person would take it."

"Maybe that's true, but I'm staying in Acorn Field Heights. I'm sorry. I don't want to be ungrateful. I know that—"

"You can't be serious." He moved closer, around the table's edge, and I stepped back on instinct. "Quinn. Think about what you're saying."

"I have thought about it." My spine hit the wall behind me. When had he gotten so close? "But I'm building something here. I have clients, I have my shop, I have—"

"What? The handyman? Really, Quinn?" His laugh scraped across my skin. "You barely know the guy. What can he possibly give you that I can't? I'm offering stability. A future. What's he got?" Another step. He was close enough now that I could smell his cologne, that expensive stuff that made the insides of my nostrils tingle. "I'm offering you a way to dig yourself out of this hole you've jumped into. A real job, real money, and you're throwing it away for some—"

"Stop." The word came out sharper than I meant it. Or maybe I had meant it. My hands had closed into fists by my sides. "Asher has nothing to do with this."

"Doesn't he?" Carter planted both hands on the worktable, looming. "Or are you just running away from everything we built because you're scared? Because being with me meant you'd actually have to show up and work instead of hiding in your little shop making princess dresses for children's birthday parties?"

The words sank in like hooks, catching on the insecurities I'd hidden about my work. For half a second, I heard them in my own voice—all those times I'd wondered if I was being childish, if I was wasting my degree, if I should want what Carter wanted instead of what made me happy.

Then I remembered Asher standing in that exact spot, watching me work on a gown with curiosity in his eyes. The way he'd asked how I sourced the antique beads, how I achieved the drape in the sleeves, how I learned to work with such delicate fabric. The way he'd listened to my answers.

"I gave you my answer. You should leave." I reached for my phone on the counter, but Carter moved faster.

His hand closed around my wrist—not squeezing, not bruising, but firm enough to make my breath catch. "No. Not until you listen to me."

"Carter, let go—"

"Just listen." His other hand came up to frame my face, thumb pressing against my jaw. Possessive. "You clearly can't see this, but you're making a mistake. I'm the one who knows what's best for you. I always have. Remember? I've always chosen the best path for you. For us. And what's best is coming back to the city, to me, to the life we planned together. This—" he gestured vaguely at the shop without releasing me "—this is a phase. A quarter-life crisis. I'm willing to forgive it if you come to your senses."

My heart hammered against my ribs. The wall was cold against my back, his body blocking the path to the door, his hand still holding my wrist like he had every right to touch me.

"Let. Go." I tried to twist away, but his grip tightened.

"Not until you promise you'll think about it. Really think about it."

"I have thought about it. My answer is no."

His face changed. The careful neutrality cracked, revealing something harder underneath. "You're being childish."

"And you're hurting me."

"I'm barely touching you." But he didn't let go. His thumb pressed harder against my jaw, tilting my face up to look at him. "This is what I'm talking about. You're so dramatic about everything. You always have been. It's why you need someone to guide you, to help you see clearly—"

The bell chimed.

Carter's hand dropped from my face but stayed locked around my wrist. I turned my head toward the door, relief flooding through me so fast it made me dizzy.

Asher stood in the doorway, white paper bag from the diner in one hand. His eyes moved from my face to Carter's hand on my wrist, and his whole body went still. Not frozen—still. Like a wolf deciding whether to attack or wait.

"Reynolds. Let go of her." His voice was quiet. Too quiet.

"This is a private conversation." Carter didn't release me. He hardly spared Asher a second glance. "You don't need to be here."

"Quinn." Asher's gaze found mine, and something in my chest loosened at the steadiness there. "You want him here?"

"I... No. I don't," I choked out.

"Then you need to leave, Reynolds." Asher set the bag down on the counter by the door. "Now."

"Oh yeah? Who do you think you are, handyman?" Carter finally turned, his grip on my wrist shifting to pull me toward him. "I told you, this doesn't concern you."

"Funny thing." Asher took one step into the shop, and I could see his hands now—relaxed at his sides but ready. "I've got a chainsaw in my truck. Real useful tool. Cuts through just about anything. Dead wood, stubborn stumps, guys who don't understand what 'no' means." His head tilted, eyes never leaving Carter's face. "Doing what I do, I happen to be really good with my hands. Won a state fair competition two years back, actually. Carved a bear out of cedar in under two hours. Bet I could work a lot faster on something less dense."

Carter's hand finally released my wrist.

"Are you threatening me?"

"I'm simply making an observation." Asher didn't smile. "About my skills. And my tools. And how quickly I can use them when something's where it doesn't belong."

I rubbed my wrist where Carter had held it. There was no mark, but I could still feel the pressure of his fingers.

Carter looked between us, his face flushing dark. "Despite his audacity, I'll give you one last chance, Quinn. I'm a nice guy. And if you don't leave with me, you're going to regret this. All of this. Him especially. When you come crawling back to the city because this fantasy falls apart, don't expect me to be waiting."

"I won't." My voice shook, but the words were solid. "The only thing I regret is not ending this sooner."

He grabbed his keys from his pocket. "You deserve each other. Small-town nobody and a girl playing dress-up. Have a nice life."

The bell chimed his exit. Through the front window, I watched him stalk to his rental car, yank the door open hard enough to make it bounce, and peel away from the curb too fast. The spiteful part of me hoped Sheriff Marx would pull him over and give him a ticket.

My legs started shaking. I locked them, willing myself to stay upright, but my hands were trembling against my thighs and my breath came too quick and shallow.

"Hey." Asher's voice was gentle now, all that dangerous stillness gone. "You're okay. He's gone."

"I know." I pressed my palms flat against the worktable. The velvet was soft under my fingers, grounding. "I'm fine."

"Quinn—"

"I'm fine." But my voice cracked on the words, betraying me.

Asher moved closer, slow and careful like I might spook. He didn't touch me, just stood near enough that I could smell sawdust and soap and something earthy. "Can I—would it be okay if I checked your wrist?"

I nodded, not trusting my voice. He took my hand in both of his, so gentle it made my throat tight, and turned it to examine where Carter had grabbed me. His fingers were rough with calluses, warm against my skin.

"No bruising," he murmured. "Does it hurt?"

"No." I watched his thumb brush across my pulse point, feather-light. "Thank you. For coming. For—" I gestured vaguely at the door. "The chainsaw thing."

His mouth curved slightly. "I probably shouldn't have threatened him. Marx would have my hide."

"It was perfect." A surprised laugh bubbled up. "Nobody's ever threatened someone with power tools for me before."

"First time for everything." He released my hand slowly, like he was giving me time to step away if I wanted. I didn't want to. "I brought pot roast. Folks at the diner made extra. I figured you'd been working too hard to remember dinner."

The smell hit me when he reached for the bag. It was rich and savory, carrots and potatoes and beef that had been cooking for hours. My stomach growled so loud we both heard it.

"When did you eat last?" he asked.

"Lunch. The turkey club you brought."

"Quinn, that was eight hours ago." He picked up the bag, pulled out the container. "Come on. Sit."

We ended up at the worktable, the pot roast between us. He'd only brought one fork, so we passed it back and forth, and somehow that felt more intimate than anything else that had happened tonight. The food was warm and comforting.

"You want me to stay?" Asher asked after we'd eaten in silence for a few minutes. "Just in case he comes back?"

I could have said no. Probably could have told him I was fine, and that I could handle this myself. Carter wasn't a threat, after all. But my hands were still shaking, and the shop felt too big and too empty, and the idea of being alone right now made something clench in my chest.

"Would you mind?" The words came out small. "I know it's late, and you probably have to be up early—"

"I'll stay as long as you need."

The relief that flooded through me was so strong it was almost embarrassing. "Thank you."

He settled into the chair across from me, stretched his legs out under the table. "So tell me about the Victorian one. You said the beading was based on actual mourning traditions?"

So I did. I told him about the research, about how Victorian mourning rituals were elaborate and specific, about the symbolism in the jet beads and the meaning behind the sleeve draping. He listened the way he always listened, asking questions that showed he was actually paying attention, and slowly the trembling in my hands subsided.

Around midnight, I went back to the mourning gown. Asher didn't leave. He just sat there while I worked, occasionally asking about technique or telling me stories about growing up on the farm. At one point, he called his older brother, double checking that the sheriff wouldn't have grounds to arrest him for hypothetically threatening a man with a chainsaw. The silence between conversations was comfortable, broken only by the soft sound of thread pulling through fabric.

"How'd you learn all this?" he asked eventually. "The historical stuff, I mean."

"Libraries, mostly. Museums. I did an internship at a costume archive in college." I tied off another bead. "Carter thought it was a waste of time. Said I should focus on modern commercial work instead of 'playing historian.'"

"Carter's an idiot."

I looked up, surprised into a laugh. "Yeah?"

"Yeah." Asher leaned back, arms crossed. "Anyone who doesn't see how good you are at this is either blind or threatened. Probably both."

A flush erupted on my cheeks and I ducked my head, focusing on the next bead to hide how much his words affected me. "He said I was being childish. Playing dress-up."

"You're running your own business doing something you're skilled at and passionate about. That's the opposite of childish." His voice was firm. "That's brave."

I threaded another bead, then another. The repetitive motion was soothing, and with Asher here the shop didn't feel lonely anymore. It felt like mine in a way it hadn't before—not just my business, but my space, my choice, my life that I was building without anyone's permission or approval.

"Asher?"

"Yeah?"

"I'm really glad you showed up when you did."

"Me too." He shifted in his chair. "For what it's worth, you handled that well. Standing your ground, I mean. That took guts."

"I was terrified."

"Being scared and doing it anyway is the definition of courage." He was quiet for a moment. "You know you can call me, right? If he comes back, or texts you, or anything."

"Okay."

We fell back into comfortable silence. I worked through the remaining beads, and Asher stayed put. By the time I tied off the final thread, it was past three in the morning and exhaustion pulled at my bones.

"Done." I held up the mourning gown, admiring how the jet beads caught the light. "What do you think?"

"It's beautiful." He stood, stretching. "You should be proud."

"I am." And I meant it.

Asher moved toward the door, and my stomach dropped at the thought of him leaving.

"I'll walk you out," I said, following him. "Make sure everything's locked."

At the door, he paused. "You going to be okay tonight?"

"Yeah." I wrapped my arms around myself. "Thank you. For everything."

"Anytime." He reached out like he might touch my arm, then seemed to think better of it. His hand dropped. "I mean that. Anytime you need someone to threaten your ex with chainsaws or just keep you company while you work, I'm here."

After he left, I locked the door and leaned against it, breathing in the lingering scent of pot roast and sawdust. My phone buzzed in my pocket.

> You're making the biggest mistake of your
> life.

Another buzz.

> I gave you everything and this is how you
> repay me?

Another.

> You'll never make it on your own.

I stared at the messages, my heart picking up speed again. Then I blocked his number, deleted the texts, and set my phone face-down on the counter.

# Chapter Eleven

## ASHER

I went home early in the morning feeling like a zombie. I showered, changed into clean clothes that didn't smell like Quinn's chamomile tea and the faint smoke from her shop's broken heater, and tried to sleep for maybe forty minutes before giving up and staring at my bedroom ceiling, replaying every moment of last night on a loop.

Quinn's hands shaking. Carter's grip on her wrist. The panic in her eyes. The way she'd looked at me when I told her I wasn't leaving. Like she couldn't quite believe someone would stay.

My phone buzzed on the nightstand. Levi's name lit up the screen with a one word text.

So?

I typed back.

She's okay. Carter left. She's safe.

I waited for his response, but he took a while.

Good. festival setup starts at noon. you
coming?

Yeah

Also for the record, threatening someone
with detailed descriptions of what you'd do
with your bare hands and a chainsaw
probably counts as assault

You said probably

I did. Just be careful.

Where's the fun in that?

I set the phone down and scrubbed both hands over my face. My
eyes felt like someone had rubbed them with sandpaper. Coffee. I
needed coffee and maybe eight more hours of sleep, but the festival
wasn't going to set itself up, and Quinn would be there. I couldn't leave
her to face the town alone after last night, not when half of Acorn Field
Heights probably already knew about Carter showing up.

Small towns. You couldn't sneeze without someone three blocks
away saying "bless you."

By the time I made it to the village green, the place was packed with
volunteers hauling tables and hammering stakes into the ground. The
sky hung low and grey, waiting with rain that the forecast swore
wouldn't hit until midnight. I didn't believe it. The air already smelled
like rain.

I found Quinn's booth near the gazebo. She wasn't there yet, but
the metal frame was already half-assembled, listing slightly to the left
where one leg hadn't been secured properly. I grabbed a mallet from the
tool pile and got to work.

"You look like death." Levi appeared beside me, holding two paper
cups that smelled like Caroline's extra-strong coffee. "Here."

I took one and drank half of it in three gulps, wincing at the bitter
taste. "Thanks."

"Quinn okay?"

"Yeah. Shaken up, but okay." I hammered the stake deeper, the impact rattling up my arms. "Carter kept calling. She text me to say she blocked him last night."

"Good." Levi checked his phone, frowning at the screen. "Amberlyn still isn't back from Boston."

"She said she'd be here, right?" I watched my older brother shrug, a furrow forming between his brows. I punched him in the shoulder, not hard, but enough to pull his attention from his phone. "She'll be here."

"Yeah." He didn't sound convinced. He shoved the phone back in his pocket and grabbed a stake from the pile. "Come on. Let's get this booth straight before it falls over."

We worked in silence for a few minutes. Levi kept checking his phone. I kept scanning the green for Quinn's car. Neither of us was subtle about it.

"You fell fast," Levi said, a ghost of a smirk on his mouth.

"Whatever."

"You like her."

It wasn't a question, but I answered anyway because I knew he was going to give me grief either way. "Yeah. I do."

He looked at me, something complicated crossing his face. "Don't mess it up. She's good people, and she's had a rough time with that ex. She deserves someone who'll show up."

"I know."

"Good." He hammered another stake, then straightened up with a grimace, rubbing the small of his back. "I'm getting too old for this."

"You're right. I'll go find you a cane," I said, ducking as he took a swing at me. "Actually, I bet I could find a walker."

"Keep laughing. You'll be hurting too when your my age." He grabbed his coffee and took a long drink. "Sawyer's coming by later. He's got the custody meeting tomorrow morning, and he's losing his mind about it."

"Do you think he's going to lose Maple?"

"I don't know. Jen's lawyer is pushing hard on the 'stable employment' angle." Levi glared at nothing in particular. "Said part-time farm work doesn't count as stable."

"That's garbage."

"Yeah, well, garbage or not, Sawyer's been frantically looking at other options. Out of state, maybe."

I hammered harder, trying to work out the frustration building in my chest. He'd left before me when our dad had his heart attack, and I'd almost chosen not to go to college because I didn't want to leave Levi alone on the farm, but Levi had insisted I go. I'd come back as soon as I graduated. Sawyer hadn't. I'd resented it for a while. Still though, the last thing I wanted was for him to lose his daughter. I knew how much that would destroy him.

"He'll figure it out," I said, even though I didn't know how.

"Yeah." Levi didn't sound like he believed it either.

He left when he got a text from Sawyer, and I finished securing Quinn's booth. just as the first drops of rain started falling. Fat and cold, they smacked against my arms and the back of my neck. Around the green, people looked up at the sky with varying degrees of alarm. Mayor Goldwin was on his phone near the gazebo, probably calling the weather service to yell at them about their terrible forecast.

"Think we should postpone?" someone asked.

"Festival's tomorrow no matter what," Goldwin called back. "But we need to secure everything tonight. Tie down what you can, cover the rest. Move!"

The rain picked up, going from scattered drops to a steady drizzle in the space of a breath. I grabbed tarps from the supply pile and started throwing them over Quinn's booth, tucking the edges under the frame to keep them from blowing away.

Thunder rumbled in the distance. Not close yet, but coming.

"Asher?"

I turned. Quinn stood at the edge of the green, her jacket pulled tight around her and her hair plastered to her face. She looked small and tired and so beautiful it made my chest ache.

"What are you doing here?" I jogged over, already shrugging out of my jacket to drape over her shoulders. "I thought you were doing last-minute decorations at the shop."

"I wanted to help with the booth, but I lost track of time." She pulled my jacket closer, and even soaked through, I could feel the warmth of her underneath. "And I wanted to thank you. For last night. For staying. For—for everything."

"You don't have to thank me."

"I do, though." She looked up at me, rain dripping off her nose and catching on her eyelashes.

Thunder cracked overhead, closer now. The wind picked up, whipping Quinn's red hair across her face and sending tarps snapping like sails. Around us, people were running for cover, abandoning booths to save themselves from the storm.

"We need to go," Levi called, already halfway to his truck. "Asher, get her out of here!"

I grabbed Quinn's hand, and we ran. The rain came down in sheets now, soaking us through in seconds. My boots slipped on wet grass, and I tightened my grip on Quinn's hand to keep her from falling. The village green turned into a blur of movement and noise, everyone scrambling to secure booths and get to safety before the storm really hit.

"My shop!" Quinn shouted over the wind. "Let's go there!"

We ran toward Main Street, dodging puddles and abandoned festival supplies. Lightning split the sky, bright enough to leave afterimages dancing across my vision. Thunder followed immediately, so loud I felt it in my bones.

She fumbled with her keys, hands shaking from cold or adrenaline or both. I steadied her fingers with mine and helped her get the key in the lock. The door swung open, and we tumbled inside as another crack of thunder shook the building.

Quinn locked the door behind us and leaned against it, breathing hard. Water dripped off both of us onto the hardwood floor, forming puddles that spread and merged. Outside, the storm raged. Inside, it was quiet except for our breathing and the steady drum of rain on the roof.

"That was wet," she said.

"Very." I was still holding her hand. Neither of us moved to let go.

She looked up at me, her eyes dark in the dim light filtering through the shop windows. "You're soaked."

"So are you."

"I have a heater in the back room. And probably some dry clothes, if you don't mind wearing a pirate shirt."

"I'm not wearing a pirate shirt."

"You already wore it once."

"I know."

"Fine. Your loss. They're very comfortable." She finally let go of my hand and walked deeper inside, leaving wet footprints in her wake. "Come on. Before you freeze to death in my shop. That would be terrible for business."

I followed her through rows of costumes hanging like ghosts in the shadows. The back room, which had seemed so large when the sunlight was streaming in the other day, felt small and cluttered with nothing but dark grey storm clouds peering in through the windows. Quinn plugged in a space heater that kicked on with a wheezing sound and she started rummaging through a box of clothes.

"Here." She tossed me a towel. "Dry off. I'll find something that won't make you look like you're about to pillage a village."

I caught the towel and watched her dig through boxes. She pulled out a plain black t-shirt and a pair of sweatpants. "These might work. They're from a modern-day costume, so no ruffles or anything."

"Thanks." I took the clothes and waited for her to turn around before stripping off my wet shirt. The heater was starting to warm the room, but my skin was still covered in goosebumps.

"Carter hasn't texted since I blocked him," Quinn said, her back still to me. "I keep checking, like I'm waiting for the other shoe to drop."

"He's not coming back." I pulled on the dry shirt. It was a size too small, but it beat hypothermia. Making sure she wasn't watching, I slipped into the sweatpants too and told her I was decent. "If he does, he'll have to go through me first." Before she could speak, I nodded towards the easel that still held my painting from before. "If you don't have a ton of work to do, I have an idea for something fun we could do during the storm." I flashed a grin at her, and when she saw the painting, a wide smile crossed her lips.

"Really?"

"Yeah."

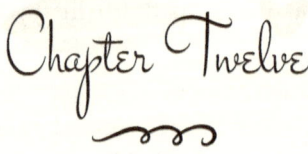

# Chapter Twelve

## ASHER

The storm was in full torrential downpour mode around eight, and by eight-thirty the power started flickering. Thunder rolled through town like it was trying to shake buildings off their foundations, and the rain sounded like someone was dumping buckets on the roof. Quinn and I stayed in the back room of her costume shop.

"Should we be worried?" Quinn asked, watching the lights flicker again.

"Probably." I wiped paint off my hands with a rag. "But we've got candles, right?"

She pointed to three pillar candles on the worktable, already lit because she was smart like that. The warm glow made everything softer, turned the cluttered workspace into something that felt safe despite what was happening outside. Lightning flashed through the windows, bright enough to hurt.

"Okay, that one was close." She wrapped her arms around herself, and I noticed she was shivering. The temperature had dropped about fifteen degrees in the last hour.

"Come here." I held out my hand, and she took it without hesitation. I pulled her close, wrapping both arms around her, feeling her relax against my chest. We stood like that for a minute, listening to the storm rage while we stayed warm in our small circle of candlelight. She fit against me like she was designed for this exact spot, and I had to resist the urge to rest my chin on top of her head.

"This is nice," she said.

"Which part? The potential apocalypse or the potential power outage?"

"The part where you're here." She tilted her head back to look at me, and the candlelight caught in her eyes.

The lights flickered one more time, staying dark for several seconds before it came back on. When it went out, though, we were left with just the candles and the occasional lightning flash through the windows. The darkness made everything feel closer, more intimate. Quinn's phone was somewhere in the front room, dead with its old battery. Mine was in my jacket pocket with about sixty percent charge.

"So, painting. Want to learn?" I asked, because standing in the dark thinking about how much I wanted to kiss her was probably not the best use of our time.

"Yes!"

"Good." I gestured toward the easel where I'd been working. "As you can see from the single painting I've done in the last several years, I'm clearly Michael Angelo. You should consider it an honor to be my student."

She laughed, and it was the best sound I'd heard all day. The kind of laugh that made her whole body shake against mine. "Okay. Teach me."

I'd left some of my supplies in her back room, including a fresh canvas. I got out paints and brushes, showed her how to mix colors on the palette. She was nervous, holding the brush awkwardly at first.

"It's just paint," I told her. "You can't break it."

"I could definitely mess it up."

"There's no such thing as messing up. Only happy accidents as my favorite mentor used to say." I stepped behind her. "Here, like this."

I wrapped my hand around hers, guiding the brush through the first stroke. She went stiff for half a second, then relaxed into the motion. Her hair tickled my jaw. My heart was doing this annoying thing where it forgot how to beat at a normal rhythm.

"Like this?" She made a broad stroke across the canvas, and I could hear the smile in her voice.

"Exactly like that." I rested my chin on her shoulder, watching her work. Big mistake. Now I could see the curve of her neck, the small freckle just below her ear. "You're already thinking like an artist. See how you're not trying to control every detail? That's good. Let the paint do some of the work."

"This is actually fun." She mixed blue and white, creating something close to the color of morning sky. At least, that's what it looked like in the candle light. In all honesty, it would likely appear a different color in true daylight. But for now, it was perfect. She was perfect.

Her elbow brushed my ribs. "I didn't think I'd be any good at this."

"You're better than good. You've got natural instinct for color and composition." I patted her shoulder gently when her brush was far enough away from the canvas, then forced myself to step back and give her space before I did something stupid. "Keep going."

But she turned around instead of going back to the canvas. "Why'd you move?"

"Because I was—" *Standing too close. Thinking about kissing you. Forgetting how to function like a normal human.* "Distracting you."

"I didn't mind."

The air between us felt charged, and not from the lightning outside. She stared at me with this expression I couldn't quite read, her lips parted, and I was about three seconds away from closing the distance between us when thunder shook the building hard enough to rattle the windows.

Quinn jumped, and I caught her hand. "It's okay. Just noise."

"That was really loud."

"Storm's right overhead." I didn't let go of her hand. She didn't pull away. "Want to keep painting, or should we just stand here and hold hands like awkward teenagers?"

She laughed again, and some of the tension broke. "Both?"

"Both works."

We stood there for a minute, her hand warm in mine, the candles throwing dancing shadows across the walls. Then she squeezed my fingers once and turned back to the canvas. I watched her work, fascinated by the concentration on her face, the way she bit her lip when she was thinking. She painted something abstract but beautiful, all blues and greens that somehow captured the feeling of the storm without trying to recreate it.

"I like this," she said after a while. "Being creative without worrying about getting it right."

"That's the secret. There is no right. Just what feels true."

She glanced at me over her shoulder. "You should teach art classes. You're good at this."

"At what? Standing in the dark watching you paint?"

"At making people feel like they can do things they didn't think they could."

Before I could figure out how to respond, the power died in a way that felt final. Not just a flicker but a surrender to the storm. Darkness surrounded us, broken only by the three candles. Lightning illuminated everything in harsh white relief for a second. Thunder followed right away, shaking the walls.

Quinn gasped, and I pulled her close again, her heart racing against my ribs. We stood frozen in the dark, listening to the wind howl and rain hammer the windows. My phone was still in my jacket pocket, but the jacket was hanging on a hook by the back door and I didn't want to let go of Quinn to get it.

"I should check if it's just us or the whole street," I said after a minute, my voice sounding loud in the quiet between thunderclaps. "Make sure this isn't something we need to worry about."

"Don't go out in this." Her hands tightened on my shirt.

"I'll just look. Two minutes, I promise." I kissed the top of her head without thinking, then froze. But she didn't pull away, just made a small sound that could have been agreement or protest or something else.

I felt my way to where I'd left my jacket. It was heavy canvas, a work jacket I wore for farm jobs, the one with paint stains and a rip in one pocket. I pulled it on, then grabbed my phone and turned on the flashlight.

Quinn looked small in the beam, surrounded by costumes and art supplies. Paint smudged on her cheek. Eyes wide.

"Be careful," she said.

"Always am."

I headed through the shop toward the front door, my phone flashlight cutting through the darkness. Outside looked like the end of the world. Rain coming down sideways, wind bending trees nearly double, leaves and debris flying past. I stepped out onto the sidewalk and got soaked in seconds despite the jacket.

The wind nearly knocked me over. I grabbed the doorframe, steadied myself, then looked down Main Street. Every building was dark. The whole block, maybe the whole town. Street lights out, no glow from windows, nothing but storm and darkness and lightning that turned everything bright before plunging it all back into black.

I was about to go back inside when I saw it.

Lightning hit the shop's roof. Not close to it, not near it—hit it with a crack so loud my ears rang. Bright white light exploded across my vision, and for a second I couldn't move, too stunned by the flash.

Then I smelled it. Smoke.

I looked up and saw orange light flickering through the front windows of the shop. My brain caught up to my body and I ran, yanking the door open, shouting Quinn's name.

"Quinn!"

"Back here!" Her voice came from the back room, confused and scared. "Asher, what's happening? Why does it smell like—"

"The shop's on fire! Lightning hit the roof!" I was already moving toward her, my flashlight bouncing wild shadows across the walls. Smoke poured in from the corner where I'd noticed the burned outlet. Not good. Not good. Not good.

I found Quinn in the back room, staring at the doorway where smoke was curling in. She had her arms full of costumes, pulling things off racks like she was trying to save inventory.

"Quinn, we need to get out!"

"Just a few more things—" She reached for another costume, a purple witch dress with silver stars.

"Now!" I grabbed her arm, but she pulled away, still trying to gather more. The smoke was making my eyes water, making it hard to breathe. Heat was building, turning the air thick.

I spotted the fire extinguisher on the wall near the bathroom. I dropped Quinn's arm and ran for it, yanking it off its mount. Pulled the pin, aimed at the doorway where flames were starting to appear, squeezed the trigger.

A pathetic spray came out. The extinguisher must have been expired, hadn't been serviced in who knew how long. The stream did nothing against the flames eating through old wood and fabric.

"We need to leave!" I threw the useless extinguisher aside and turned back to Quinn. She was still trying to save things, tears streaming down her face, coughing. I dialed Sheriff Marx, but the call didn't go through. When I check the top corner of my phone, it showed I had no signal. I cursed under my breath.

An ember must've caught my jacket sleeve. I didn't register it at first. Not until pain flared hot on my skin, the smell of burning fabric mixed with smoke. I shouted and ripped the jacket off, threw it on the floor where it burned. Now I was just in a t-shirt, and the heat was everywhere, pressing in.

Flames blocked the path to the front door. The back exit was our only option, but Quinn didn't seem to understand that. She was still trying to save one more costume, one more piece of inventory.

"Quinn, now!" I grabbed her hand and pulled her toward the back exit. She stumbled, dropped the costumes, finally seemed to understand how serious this was.

We pushed through smoke so thick I couldn't see the door. My lungs burned, my eyes streamed, and Quinn was coughing so hard she couldn't walk. I found the back door handle, slammed it open, and we stumbled out into the rain and wind.

The cold air came as a relief. We both bent over, gasping and coughing, rain soaking through our clothes in seconds. Behind us, orange light glowed through windows, smoke pouring into the night sky despite the storm.

I pulled Quinn into my arms and she collapsed against me, shaking and crying and clinging like I was the only solid thing left. I was shivering hard now, the wet t-shirt doing nothing against the cold, but I didn't care. She was safe. We were both safe.

"It's okay," I told her, even though nothing was okay. "You're okay. We're okay."

She was sobbing now, full body shaking, and all I could do was hold her in the rain while her shop burned. Lightning kept flashing, illuminating her face in harsh white light, and I could see the devastation in her eyes. This shop was everything to her. Her dream, her investment, her future.

And it was gone. Just gone.

"This town really is cursed, isn't it?"

The voice cut through the storm from behind us. Every muscle in my body went rigid. I knew that voice. I'd hoped to never hear it again.

I glanced up to see Carter standing about twenty feet away, hands in his pockets. Just standing in the rain, not helping, not calling for help. Watching. Just watching us struggle, watching the shop burn, watching Quinn fall apart.

# Chapter Thirteen

## QUINN

I clung to Asher like he was the only thing keeping me upright. Pretty sure he was. Cold rain pounded down on us, and I felt him shivering under my grip. Beside us, my shop burned. Orange light flickered across the flooding pavement, throwing shadows that danced and twisted. Bitter smoke mixed with rain.

"I bet you wish you took my offer now, don't you?"

I went still. Carter. Carter was here. My hands tightened on Asher's arms, nails digging in. How long had he been watching? Why was he here now, during the fire? Why wouldn't he leave me alone.

Asher's whole body was tense against mine. He stepped to the side, putting himself between me and Carter like a wall. He shouted to be heard over the storm.

"You need to leave, Reynolds. Now."

Carter acted like Asher didn't exist. He looked past him, around him, focused directly on me like Asher was just some inconvenient obstacle blocking his view. The dismissal was so complete it would've been funny if it wasn't so infuriating.

"Quinn, look at this." Carter gestured at the burning building. His voice went gentle, concerned, the tone he always used when he was about to explain why his way was better. "Your shop is gone. You have no reason to stay now."

Rain dripped from his hair, ran down his face. He wore an expensive rain jacket. Everything about him screamed city, screamed the life he kept insisting I wanted.

"Come back with me. Tonight." He took a step closer. Asher shifted with him, maintaining the distance. "We can be gone before sunrise. Start fresh. Put all this behind us."

"No." Despite the tears streaming down my face. Despite the fact that everything I'd worked for was turning to ash in front of me. Despite the fact that I was sleep deprived, tired, and soaking wet. I spoke the word clearly.

Carter blinked. Paused. Then continued like I hadn't spoken. "If you'd just listen—"

"I said no." I stepped around Asher, stood beside him instead of behind him. "I'm not listening to you anymore."

Carter's mouth tightened. Just a little. Just enough to show his frustration. "You're not thinking clearly. You're in shock. You've just lost everything—"

"I'm thinking perfectly clearly." My voice remained steady. "I'm staying here."

He shook his head, did that thing where he pinched the bridge of his nose like I was being unreasonable. Like I was a child who didn't understand what was good for her.

"What's keeping you here?" He spread his hands, gestured at the burning building, at the rain-soaked street, at this whole dying town he'd looked down on. "This burned building? This place that can't even keep the power on during a storm?"

I reached for Asher's hand. Found it waiting. Our fingers slid together, locked tight. His palm was cold from the rain but solid, real, here.

"Him." I looked at Carter when I said it. Wanted him to see my face, hear the certainty in my voice. "He's my reason to stay."

Carter actually laughed. It was a short, bitter sound. "You hardly know him, Quinn. This is just a rebound. You're hurt and confused and latching onto the first guy who—"

"I look forward to knowing him more every day." I squeezed Asher's hand. He squeezed back, and his warmth spread through my palm, giving me the strength I needed to continue. "Every single day."

Carter took a step forward. Asher's grip tightened on mine.

"You're throwing away everything we built—"

"We didn't build anything." The words came fast now. "You controlled everything. Where we lived, where we worked, who we saw, what I wore to your company parties. That's not building, Carter. That's just you arranging things how you wanted them. I was just a doll for you to play future with."

"That's not—I was helping you become the best version of—"

"Of you." I cut him off again. It felt good, taking that power back. "The best version of you. Not me. This is the best version of m-me." I choked. It wasn't on purpose, but my eyes burned from tears and smoke and the knowledge that if I stayed, I'd have to start over with no money. With nothing.

Not nothing, though. I had Asher.

Carter took another step forward. Not quite threatening, but close. Testing boundaries he had no right to test anymore.

Asher let go of my hand.

For a second I panicked—was he leaving? Did I push too far, claim too much? But he just crouched down, fiddling with his boot laces or something. Now? He was dealing with his shoes now?

"I want you to leave, Carter. I'm not going with you. I'm staying. You told me to make a decision. It's not my fault you can't accept it." I lifted my chin, blinking back rain and tears.

"No, Quinn, I'm not going to—"

Asher stood back up, but his hand wasn't empty like it had been a second ago. Now there was an object. A hammer.

I blinked. Stared. Had no idea where it came from. It must've been on the ground, left by someone earlier, but the casual way Asher flipped it in his palm made it look deliberate. Planned. He tossed it up, caught it, let the weight settle in his grip.

Carter stared at the hammer. At Asher. Back to the hammer.

"Quinn, please." His voice shifted, went back to that reasonable tone. That sad, concerned voice that used to make me fold. "Be reasonable. Think about your future—"

"I think it's time for you to leave." Asher's voice stayed calm. Almost friendly. He flipped the hammer again, casual as anything. "Right now."

The silence that followed felt like the longest five seconds of my life. Carter looked between us, must've seen me standing shoulder to shoulder with Asher, must've noticed the hammer flipping in Asher's hand, must've realized that he'd lost whatever ground he thought he had.

"You'll regret this, Quinn." His voice went cold, all pretense of concern dropping away. "When this town swallows you whole, when you're stuck here with nothing and no one, don't call me."

"I won't need to." I stepped closer to Asher, felt his arm come around my shoulders. "I have everything I need right here."

Carter stared at me for a long moment. Rain poured down his face, dripped off his chin. Then he turned and walked away, back into the darkness and the storm. I watched until I couldn't see him anymore, until he was just another shadow swallowed by rain.

Asher dropped the hammer back on the ground. It landed with a dull thunk on the wet pavement.

At that exact moment, sirens wailed in the distance. Getting closer. Red and blue lights flashed through the rain, painting everything in alternating colors. The volunteer fire department. Finally. I didn't know who had called them, and I didn't care.

The truck pulled up and people started pouring out. The firefighters got to work, hauling hoses and shouting instructions.

Asher and I stepped back to give them room. He was shaking harder now, the adrenaline wearing off and the cold setting in. His borrowed shirt was plastered to his skin, his hair dripping into his eyes.

I turned and hugged him. Just wrapped my arms around him and held on tight while the rain poured down and the firefighters worked.

"Thank you." My voice cracked. "For everything. For saving me, for standing with me, for—"

"Always," he said into my hair, simple and certain. Like there was never any other option.

I was crying again, couldn't hold it back anymore.

It took a while, but the firefighters finally got the flames under control. They told us the were working on hot spots and making sure nothing spread.

We moved further back, out of the way. Stood there wrapped in blankets, watching the firefighters work. Steam rose from the building where water hit hot wood. The smell of smoke coated my throat, my lungs, my clothes, my hair.

"Everything I worked for." The words came out hollow. My shop, my inventory, my displays, my dreams of building something here—all of it gone. Turned to ash and smoke and ruined wood.

Asher pulled me closer. "I'll help you rebuild. With proper wiring this time."

It was such a practical thing to say. Such an Asher thing to say. I laughed despite the tears, despite everything. The sound came out wet and choked.

"Inspection-approved wiring?"

"The best inspection-approved wiring." The corner of his mouth tipped up. "It pays to date a handyman."

The humor contrasted strangely against the tragedy, but it helped. Made this survivable instead of insurmountable. We'd rebuild. Together. Not me alone, scrambling to fix everything by myself. We'd do it together because Asher believed in me.

# Chapter Fourteen

## ASHER

At six in the morning, I gave up on sleep. Two nights awake and my body was done pretending it could function, but Quinn needed help boarding up her shop, and I'd promised to be there by half past. I hauled myself out of bed and headed to Main Street, where debris littered the road like confetti after a parade nobody wanted. Broken branches, shredded banners, pumpkins split open and rotting in the gutters.

Quinn's shop looked worse in daylight. Fire had turned the brick black around the windows, and water damage warped the doorframe. I grabbed boards from my truck along with my toolbox, the wood cold against my palms.

The fire inspector was already there, clipboard in hand, walking through the damage with Quinn trailing behind him. Her hair was pulled back in a knot, and she wore the same clothes from last night. She looked small standing in the wreckage of her dream.

"The lightning strike caused the electrical fire," the inspector said, marking something on his clipboard. "Old wiring couldn't handle the surge."

Quinn nodded, arms wrapped tight around herself.

"Could have been prevented with updated electrical systems." The inspector tapped his pen against the board. "Good news is the structure's sound. Some inventory can be salvaged."

"And the bad news?" Quinn's voice came out thin.

"Can't use the space until it's inspected and cleared. Probably looking at two to three weeks minimum before any remodeling can happen."

I took mental notes about the repairs needed while the inspector listed them off. Rewiring, drywall replacement, new windows, ventilation system inspection. The list grew and so did the weight in my chest thinking about what this would cost her.

After the inspector left, Quinn went inside to assess what she could save. I watched her from the doorway, not announcing myself yet. She moved through the shop touching each ruined costume like she was saying goodbye. A sequined witch hat, smoke-damaged beyond repair. A vampire cape with the hem burned away. Kids' costumes that would never make another child smile.

Her shoulders shook, and I knew she was crying even though she tried to hide it.

I set down my tools and walked up behind her. Didn't say anything. Just turned her around gently and pulled her into a hug.

She broke against my chest, her hands gripping my shirt while she sobbed. I held her, one hand in her hair, the other spread across her back. Sometimes words just got in the way of what mattered, so I stayed quiet and let her cry.

After a while, her breathing steadied. I rested my chin on top of her head. "The important part is that you're safe."

She nodded against my chest. "I know."

"We'll figure out the rest." I meant it. Whatever it took, we'd rebuild this place. I'd rebuild it for her with my bare hands, though that would take signficantly longer than with tools.

She pulled back, wiping her eyes with the heel of her hand. "I need to sort through what I can save for the booth anyway. The festival's today."

"I'm going to board up the windows, but will you be okay here for a bit?" I brushed a strand of hair from her face. "I need to help Levi set up

Aunt Caroline's booth. It was pretty well destroyed, and she's not supposed to do heavy lifting."

"I'll be fine." She managed a weak smile that didn't reach her eyes. "Go. Your aunt needs you."

I kissed her forehead, let my lips linger there for a moment. "I'll come back and check on you soon."

Walking away from her felt wrong.

I found Levi at Aunt Caroline's booth on the village green, setting up tables for her café's festival display. He looked as exhausted as I felt, which was saying something. His hair stuck up in about five different directions, and his eyes were bloodshot.

"So you drove three hours out to get Amberlyn in the middle of the storm?" I asked, grabbing one end of a table. Both of my brother's messages, along with a few others, came in early this morning. Apparently I'd missed quite a bit during the fire, including the fact that my oldest brother had driven hours for a girl and my middle brother had spent multiple hours searching for my niece, who had run away from her mother during the storm.

Levi just nodded his head. We worked in silence for a bit, the way we always had. The Thatcher brothers weren't big talkers when things got hard. Well, maybe Sawyer was, but Levi and I leaned more towards silence.

Aunt Caroline showed up with her bitter coffee, and started fussing right away. "How's Quinn? I heard about the fire."

"She's managing." I took the coffee, let the warmth seep into my cold hands while avoiding taking any real sips. "She sorting through the damage now."

"That poor girl." Aunt Caroline pulled her jacket tighter around her. "First that ex of hers shows up, now this. But she's tough. She'll bounce back."

I hoped so. My attention kept drifting down Main Street toward Quinn's shop, worry gnawing at me about leaving her alone too long.

My phone stayed silent in my pocket. No messages from Quinn, but that wasn't surprising. Her phone had burned up in the fire. I pulled my phone out anyway, checked the screen just in case. Nothing.

We fixed up Aunt Caroline's booth surprisingly quickly, and I wiped the back of my hand over my sweaty forehead. Aunt Caroline was in tears as she thanked us, and I nodded.

"I'm going back to Quinn's. Make sure she's really okay. I'll help with the Thatcher booth later, Lee. Let me know if you hear from Sawyer about the custody meeting."

Levi grunted something that might have been acknowledgment while wrestling with a banner that kept trying to wrap itself around his head.

I headed back toward Main Street, picking up my pace when Quinn's shop came into view. There was a crowd gathered outside. My stomach dropped. I broke into a jog, scenarios running through my head. Another fire. Carter came back. Something collapsed.

But as I got closer, I realized the crowd wasn't panicking. They were carrying things. Dolores had a clothing rack loaded with vintage clothes. Art from the hardware store hauled boxes of Halloween accessories. Mayor Goldwin directed traffic like he was conducting an orchestra of community goodwill. Anna from Aunt Caroline's café had set up a table covered with pastries and thermoses of coffee. "For the volunteers," she said when she saw me staring.

"What's going on?"

"What's it look like?" She handed me a cinnamon roll. "We heard Quinn needed help. Can't have the festival without costumes, can we?"

I pushed through the crowd, looking for Quinn. Found her standing in the middle of it all, overwhelmed and crying again. But these were different tears. Happy ones.

People kept arriving. The teenager who worked at Levi's farm sometimes brought a box of fabric scraps. The owner of the antique shop donated props and decorations.

"We take care of our own," Mayor Goldwin said, hanging costumes on a temporary rack someone had set up.

Quinn kept trying to thank everyone, but her voice kept breaking. She hugged strangers, laughed and cried at the same time, and I'd never seen anything more beautiful.

When she saw me, she waved, a watery smile on her face. I waved back, putting my hands in my pockets and grinning at her from across the crowd.

Mayor Goldwin revealed a hand-painted sign: "Enchanted Threads." The gold letters caught the morning sun, and Quinn choked on tears as she hugged the mayor.

By afternoon, Quinn's booth was complete. Mismatched but beautiful. Better than anything Quinn could have built alone or with me.

The festival opened. Crowds arrived, drawn by the music and the smell of cider and fried dough. Well, that and the copious amounts of social media marketing that Amberlyn Avery had created.

I noticed something right away. People kept going to Quinn's booth first. They'd heard about the fire. Everyone knew the story.

"We heard what happened," a woman said, buying a witch costume for her daughter. "Wanted to help you rebuild."

"Saw the fire trucks last night," an older man added, renting a vampire cape. "Glad you're okay. Here's a little extra."

He handed Quinn a twenty for a ten-dollar rental.

This happened over and over. People buying things they didn't need, renting costumes for parties they weren't throwing, pressing money into Quinn's hands with quiet words of support. The booth became the story of the festival.

Quinn was in her element now. The grief from this morning had been replaced by pure joy. She talked to customers, helped kids pick costumes, made everyone feel special. I ran the photo part of the photo-booth, though she continually stole my attention. Her hands moved while she talked, gesturing and pointing, and her laugh carried across the green.

She was the complete opposite of me. I was quiet, kept to myself, processed things internally. Quinn was bubbly and chatty and connected with people without effort. She filled rooms with light while I was more comfortable in corners. But watching her shine didn't make me want to dim her. It made me want to be the person who got to see all that light up close. Who got to come home to her stories about customers and costumes and community. Who got to be the quiet to her loud, the steady to her sparkle.

Late afternoon, the photobooth hit a lull. Most people were wandering toward the food vendors or watching the scarecrow contest. I

114

looked at Quinn. She was swamped with customers, laughing at something a kid just said.

An idea hit me. Terrible idea. Embarrassing idea. But the kind of idea that felt right anyway.

I waited until she was busy with a family, then snuck over to her booth. Browsed through the costumes she'd organized on racks. Found a Victorian gentleman's outfit complete with top hat and brass-handled cane. It was ridiculous. Perfect.

I changed behind a curtain she'd set up as a makeshift dressing room, checking my reflection in a hand mirror someone donated. The costume actually fit pretty well. I adjusted the cravat, settled the top hat at the right angle, and stepped out.

Quinn was finishing with a customer. She handed over a carefully wrapped package, accepted payment, thanked them for their support. Then she turned.

And froze.

Her mouth dropped open. She laughed, the sound bright and surprised and delighted.

I adopted a British accent, complete with formal posture and everything. "Pardon me, miss, but I find myself in urgent need of a photograph with you."

She was trying not to laugh now, her hand pressed to her mouth. "Sir, I'm supposed to be working."

"This is urgent business, I assure you." I held out my hand. "It simply cannot wait."

"Well, if it's urgent..." She took my hand, still grinning.

Aunt Caroline appeared from nowhere with her phone. "Oh, I'm getting this. Don't you two move."

I kept the accent, suggesting various ridiculous poses while Quinn laughed so hard she could barely stand straight. Other festival-goers stopped to watch, pulling out their own phones.

"On three," Aunt Caroline said, holding up her phone. "One, two—"

On three, I kissed Quinn.

She gasped against my mouth, surprised, then melted into it. I felt her smile, tasted her laughter. My hand cupped her face while cameras clicked around us, but I didn't care who was watching. This was the moment. This was us.

When we broke apart, she was flushed and grinning, her fingers still gripping my ridiculous cravat. "That's going to be a great photo."

I dropped the accent, went back to my normal quiet voice. "That was the plan."

Her eyes went soft. "You're full of surprises, Asher Thatcher."

"I have my moments." I adjusted my top hat, self-conscious with half the town watching us. "Should probably get back to work."

"Probably." But she didn't let go of my cravat yet. "Thank you."

"M'lady," I said, giving her a dramatic bow as I took her hand and kissed her knuckles.

The festival continued around us. Music from the bandstand, laughter from the game booths, the smell of cider and cinnamon sugar churros. Quinn went back to helping customers. I headed to the photo-booth, still wearing the Victorian costume because taking it off felt like breaking the spell.

Besides, Quinn beamed at me every time she looked. Yeah, I wasn't taking it off.

# Chapter Fifteen

## QUINN

**FIVE MONTHS LATER**

March in Acorn Field Heights was, to my dismay, surprisingly cold as I fussed with the key in the shop door. The new jacket I'd gotten Asher for Christmas was draped over my work chair, which meant he'd probably stayed late working on the shop again last night and left his jacket, or somehow woken up earlier than me. Considering the fact that it was six am, I hoped it was the former.

I had on thick socks and a hoodie and was still shivering. The shop was freezing, but through the back room door, the space heater was humming and the smell coffee filled the air. When I pushed the door open, he was already there on a ladder with his back to me, running new wire through the ceiling while humming off-key to whatever song was stuck in his head.

"You're here early," I said.

He glanced down, and his whole face softened when he saw me. "Wanted to finish this section before the inspector comes tomorrow."

We'd spent nearly every day like this as soon as we'd gotten the green light to start reconstruction. The shop had become our routine—me handing him tools, him explaining building codes in that quiet, patient way of his, both of us covered in sawdust and paint by the end of each day.

I poured myself coffee from the thermos he'd brought and settled onto the floor with my planning notebook, which had approximately thirteen different sketches of the new layout, each one progressively more elaborate. Most of the interior had to be torn out because it was unstable, but the brick foundation remained. The new framing and walls were up and mostly insulated now. Just needed drywall. The electrical was nearly done. Plumbing went in last week.

"How's that corner coming?" I asked.

"Good. Better than before." He twisted a wire nut, tested the connection. "This whole system is going to be safer. Inspection-approved wiring, proper gauge cables, the works."

"You want breakfast?" I asked. "Aunt Caroline sent over muffins yesterday. I saved you the blueberry ones."

"In a minute." He finished the connection, climbed down the ladder with confidence I absolutely never had when climbing the death traps, and crossed to where I sat. He crouched next to me, exhaustion played around his eyes that he tried to hide. "Let me see what you're planning."

I showed him my latest sketch of the new layout. Display cases here, checkout counter there, a small seating area by the window where people could wait while I worked on rush alterations. I'd added about forty details since yesterday's version.

"I like it." He traced the counter with one finger. "You could run power here for a sewing machine if you wanted a working station up front. Let customers watch you work."

"Really? That wouldn't be too complicated?"

"Nope. Just need to add another outlet." He pulled a pencil from behind his ear—he always kept one there now, which I found unreasonably attractive—and marked the spot on my drawing. "Easy fix."

This was what mornings had become. Coffee and planning, his quiet competence next to my endless ideas, both of us building something better than what had burned down.

By noon, we'd made real progress. The wiring was all but done, walls were primed, and I'd painted the trim around two windows while

Asher installed new light fixtures. We moved around each other without colliding. The March light coming through the windows was thin and cold, but the space heater kept our corner warm enough that I'd shed my hoodie hours ago.

"Lunch?" he asked, wiping his hands on his jeans, which were already streaked with grim and dust.

"Please. I'm starving."

He unpacked sandwiches, and we sat on the floor eating them; there was only one chair and a table covered in tools. Besides, the floor was our routine.

"Levi called," Asher said between bites. "Wanted to know if we're coming to dinner at the farm on Sunday."

"Did you tell him yes?"

"Told him we'd bring dessert." He glanced at me. "That okay?"

"Of course." I leaned against his shoulder.

"Maple won't stop talking about the princess dress you made for her birthday party." He kissed the top of my head, then went back to his sandwich. "Sawyer's bringing her and Isla on Sunday. Should be chaotic."

"Maple chaos is the best kind of chaos."

We finished eating, and Asher went back to checking outlet boxes while I started painting the back wall a soft cream color that made the room feel bigger. I lost myself in the rhythm of brush strokes until I heard a knock at the front door that made us both jump.

"Quinn? Asher? You here?" Mayor Goldwin's voice echoed through the space.

I set down my brush and headed to the front, where the mayor stood in the doorway with his coat buttoned up against the cold, wearing an expression that could only be described as gleeful.

"Hi, Mayor. We weren't expecting you."

"Just wanted to check on progress." He peered past me into the shop, taking in the half-finished walls and construction supplies scattered everywhere. "Coming along nicely, I see."

Asher appeared from the back room, wiping his hands on a rag. "Everything okay, Mayor?"

"More than okay." Mayor Goldwin's smile widened into something that made my stomach flip with either hope or dread. "I have some news for you both."

"Oh?" I raised an eyebrow as Asher stepped closer.

"Well, I pulled some strings with my old company, and the insurance came through. Full coverage for the rebuild."

I stared at him. "What?"

"Full coverage. The shop rebuild is fully funded." He rocked back on his heels, clearly enjoying the look on my face and the fact that my knees had gone weak.

"Full?" My voice came out higher than normal, almost squeaky. "That's... That's incredible."

"Yup." He chuckled. "Congratulations, Quinn. You've both worked hard for this."

I turned to Asher. He was grinning, eyes bright, and before I could think about it, I launched myself into his arms. He caught me easily, always did, and spun me while I laughed and maybe cried a little, and Mayor Goldwin was chuckling somewhere behind us.

"We can reopen by summer," I said against Asher's neck. "We're going to make it."

"Told you we would." He set me down but kept his arms wrapped tight around me, like he wasn't ready to let go yet.

"Ahem." Mayor Goldwin cleared his throat with exaggerated politeness.

"Sorry," I said, not remotely sorry.

"Don't apologize. Young love and all that." He adjusted his coat, preparing to leave. "Oh, Asher, give Levi my congratulations on his engagement to Ms. Avery, would you?"

Asher nodded, still holding me. "Will do. About time he made it official."

"I certainly agree." He headed toward the door, then paused with his hand on the handle, turning back with that knowing smile that made him look like he had a secret. "You know, it sounds like there may be another engagement to celebrate soon, if Maple is a trustworthy messenger, that is."

I glanced at Asher, who had become intensely interested in a spot on the ceiling. His lips pressed together, inching upwards. A little tell he had when he was trying not to smile.

"Sounds like the Thatcher men might have quite the year next year." Mayor Goldwin winked and opened the door, letting in a blast of cold air. "Keep up the good work, you two."

The door closed behind him, leaving us in sudden silence broken only by the space heater's hum and that loose shingle still flapping overhead. I turned in Asher's arms to face him.

"Sawyer too?" I asked.

"Maple talks a lot." He shrugged, amusement dancing in his eyes. "Who knows what she's saying to people."

"Asher."

"Hmm?"

"Is there something you want to tell me?"

"Nope." But he was fighting a full smile now, losing the battle. "Just that the wiring needs to be inspected before we can do drywall in the back."

I laughed and shook my head. "Your niece has quite the imagination."

"She really does." He touched my face, thumb brushing my cheekbone. "I should get back to work. Lots to do before tomorrow."

"Right. Work." I kissed him quickly, then pulled away before I forgot about painting entirely.

The afternoon passed in comfortable silence broken by occasional questions about paint colors or outlet placement. I kept glancing at Asher while he worked, watching the way he double-checked every connection. He caught me staring once and raised an eyebrow, mouth tipping up, and I went back to my painting with heat in my cheeks.

"Hey Quinn," Asher called from the back room around four-thirty. "Can you bring me my water bottle please?"

"Be right there."

I swiped his water bottle off the table, my thoughts still caught on whether the seating area should have two chairs or three. Maybe four? But that might crowd the space. Although if people were waiting for alterations or for someone to try a costume on, they'd want somewhere comfortable to sit. I could move the display case six inches to the left, which would give me room for—

I pushed open the back room door.

Asher was on one knee in the middle of the floor.

My brain short-circuited. The water bottle slipped from my fingers and hit the ground with a hollow thunk, rolling across the concrete to bump against his boot. He didn't move to pick it up. Just stayed there on one knee, holding a small velvet box open in his hands, and inside was a ring that caught the light and threw tiny rainbows across the unfinished walls.

"Asher—" My voice came out as barely a whisper.

"Hi." His mouth tipped up, but his eyes were serious. Nervous. "So, uh, I hope Maple didn't ruin this by talking to the mayor."

I pressed my hand to my mouth, trying to remember how to breathe.

"I've been practicing what to say for two weeks." He took a breath. "But everything I came up with sounded wrong. Too flowery or too stiff or just... not me."

"You don't have to—"

"Let me try anyway." He shifted his weight, and I noticed his hands were shaking. "Quinn, I'm not the guy who makes big speeches. You know that."

"I do."

His smile got a little wider. "I know you do. Which is one of about a thousand reasons I want to marry you."

My heart stopped. Just completely stopped.

"I want to wake up every morning and know I get to spend the day watching you come up with incredible costumes. I want to hand you paintbrushes and watch you create beautiful things. I want to be the person you turn to when you're excited about a new idea, even if it's three in the morning and that idea involves seventeen different layout sketches."

I laughed through the tears that were already spilling down my cheeks.

"I want to build things with you. Not just shops, but a whole life. I want messy kitchens and Sunday dinners with you and my family. I want to be standing next to you when you reopen this place, and I want to still be standing next to you fifty years from now when some young couple asks us how we made it work."

He paused, and when he spoke again, his voice was quieter. More vulnerable. "I want every day with you, Quinn. The hard days and the easy days and all the normal, boring, perfect days in between. I want to be your person, and I want you to be mine." He held up the ring box a little higher. "So... will you marry me?"

"Yes." The word burst out of me before he even finished the question. "Yes, yes, of course yes."

He stood and slid the ring onto my finger, and his hands were definitely shaking now, and so were mine. The ring fit perfectly—a vintage band with a small diamond that looked like it belonged to someone's grandmother.

"My brother's helped me pick it out," Asher murmured, watching me stare at it. "We made a day of ring shopping." His thumb traced over my knuckles. "I didn't need a full day like them, though. Took me about five minutes to realize this was the perfect one."

"Asher." I threw my arms around his neck, and he caught me, lifting me off the ground and spinning me the way he had earlier.

When he set me down, I kissed him.

"I love you," I whispered when we finally pulled apart. "I love you so much."

"I love you too." He kissed my forehead, my cheeks, the tip of my nose. Asher tucked a strand of hair behind my ear. "Mom would've loved you. The way you care about people, the way you're always trying to make things beautiful. She would've loved that you're brave enough to start over when things fall apart."

"I'm not that brave."

"You're the bravest person I know." He said it simply, like it was just a fact. "You came to a new town alone and built a business from nothing. When it burned down, you didn't give up. You just started building again. That's brave, Quinn."

I rested my forehead against his chest, feeling his steady heart beating beneath my cheek.

"When did you plan this?" I asked. "The water bottle was very smooth, by the way."

"Maple's idea, actually. She helped me practice." He laughed. "She made me do it six times until I stopped fumbling with the ring box. Also made me promise she could be a flower girl."

"She can definitely be a flower girl." I pulled back to look at him. He was beaming. I laughed and wiped my eyes, which were still leaking tears despite the fact that I couldn't stop smiling. "Fall wedding?"

"Whatever you want. I'm just happy you said yes."

I twisted the ring on my finger, watching the light dance. "After the shop reopens. That way I won't be completely stressed about timelines."

"Autumn is perfect." He wrapped his arms around me, and we stood there in the half-finished back room while March wind rattled the windows. "Though honestly, I'd marry you tomorrow in this room surrounded by paint cans if you wanted."

"Tempting, but I think Maple would riot if she didn't get to wear a princess dress and carry flowers."

"Fair point."

We sank to the floor together, our backs against the wall, my head on his shoulder and his arm around me. The space heater glowed orange beside us, and through the doorway, I could see the front room with its primed walls and new windows, all the progress we'd made together over these past months.

"I told Levi I was proposing today, and he's probably already told the whole farm, and Sawyer definitely already told Isla, who probably already told half the town."

I laughed. "So basically everyone knows except me?"

"Maple might've mentioned it to a few people. Like forty people. At church. Loudly. I was surprised you didn't hear it." He rubbed the back of his neck. "Mayor Goldwin's been winking at me for two weeks, and the fact that he stopped in here. I can't believe you didn't notice that he was blatantly staring at your left hand the entire time. He is not subtle."

"I was a bit distracted, but that explains so much." I snuggled closer. "I can't believe you've been carrying this secret around while we've been working."

"Nearly told you about it sixteen times. Especially last Tuesday when you got paint in your hair and didn't notice for three hours." His fingers traced patterns on my shoulder. "You looked so happy. Just painting and humming and planning, and I almost just blurted it out right there."

"Why didn't you?"

"I wanted it to be special. Wanted to do it right." He pulled back to meet my eyes. "You deserve the big moment, Quinn. The romance and the surprise and all of it."

"This is perfect." I touched his face, stubble scratching my palm. "Exactly perfect."

Asher raised my hand to his mouth and kissed my knuckles. "I love you, Quinn. Now let's get your dream shop ready to pass inspection."

# Read the First Chapter in Maggie's First Christmas Romcom Novella

# MAGGIE ELLIS

# The Christmas Cabin Mix-Up

A CUTE HOLIDAY NOVELLA

# Chapter 1

Mandatory vacation. Two words that shouldn't exist together in the English language, yet here I was, stuffing my meticulously organized suitcase into the back of my Subaru while cursing Steven's name under my breath.

"Take the time off for the holidays, Daisy, or I'll make the decision for you." His words echoed in my head as I triple-checked my GPS route to the middle of nowhere. As if I was some kind of workaholic who needed an intervention. I mean, sure, I hadn't taken a sick day in three years, and yes, I did answer emails during my lunch breaks, but that was called being dedicated. Apparently, Steven called it "concerning behavior that requires immediate attention."

What Steven didn't understand was that work was the only thing that kept my brain from spinning into the dark places it liked to visit when I had too much free time. The places where car accidents replayed on loop and every unexpected sound made me jump. Two years since the last time, and I still couldn't drive in the rain without my hands shaking. The screech of brakes, the explosion of glass, the way my world had literally turned upside down in the space of three seconds. Those memories lived just beneath the surface, waiting for any moment of stillness to resurface.

He said I needed the break because I worked too hard. What he really meant was that I needed the week to prove I could handle downtime without falling apart completely.

Didn't matter that I preferred to work on Christmas when everyone else was taking a break. It meant less people to deal with.

I sighed.

The drive up the mountain took longer than expected, partly because of the snow that had started falling around mile marker fifteen, and partly because I kept stopping to reorganize my emergency kit. Every time I heard the crunch of gravel under my tires or felt the car slide slightly on a curve, my chest would tighten and I'd have to pull over until my breathing returned to normal.

By the time I reached the turnoff for Pinecrest Road, my knuckles were white from gripping the steering wheel, and I was questioning every life choice that had led me to driving up a mountain in winter conditions.

I hated mountain roads. I hated driving in snow. I especially hated driving in snow on mountain roads where one wrong turn could send you careening into a ravine, just like—

No. Nope. I wasn't going there.

The cabin appeared through the trees like something out of a magazine spread. All rustic wood and stone, with icicles hanging from the eaves and smoke curling from the chimney.

I slammed on the brakes.

Smoke from the chimney?

I parked and stared at the building, my brain struggling to process what I was seeing. The rental listing had definitely said the place would be empty. Clean and ready for occupancy, but empty. Smoke suggested occupancy. Smoke suggested people.

People were not part of the plan. A vacation was bad enough. A vacation with people was torture.

I grabbed my phone to call the rental company. No signal, naturally. Because apparently, the universe had decided that my week of isolation needed to start with a mystery.

Fine. I'd handle this like I handled everything else; with logic, determination, and a healthy dose of righteous indignation. I grabbed my bags and marched up to the front door, already composing the strongly worded email I'd send as soon as I got back to civilization.

The key turned easily in the lock, which was the first thing that had gone right all day. I stepped inside, ready to confront whoever had invaded my sanctuary, and immediately froze.

The smell hit me first. Coffee and bacon and something warm that might have been cinnamon rolls. Then the sound of Christmas music drifting from somewhere deeper in the cabin, and the unmistakable clatter of someone cooking in the kitchen. Christmas lights twinkled around the ceiling, and a small Christmas tree sat in the entry room.

"Hello?" I called out, setting down my bags with more force than necessary.

"In here!" came a cheerful male voice. "Hope you're hungry. I made way too much food!"

I followed the voice toward the kitchen, my heart hammering. The rental listing had definitely said I'd have the place to myself. I'd specifically chosen this cabin because it was supposed to be sans people.

I rounded the corner into the kitchen and stopped dead.

A tall, broad-shouldered man in a flannel shirt was standing at the stove with his back to me, wielding a spatula with the confidence of someone who clearly belonged here. He glanced over his shoulder with a warm smile, and I got my first good look at brown eyes, messy hair, and the kind of easy grin that belonged in a coffee commercial.

My stomach did something entirely inappropriate.

"Perfect timing," he said, turning back to the stove. "The bacon's just finished, and I've got pancakes keeping warm in the oven. Coffee's fresh, and I found some real maple syrup in the pantry. I figured the least I could do was make a proper welcome breakfast."

"Welcome breakfast?"

"Well, yeah. You must be the owner, right? Ezra from the rental company said you might stop by to check on things." He finally turned around fully, spatula still in hand, and his smile faltered slightly. "You are Hanna, aren't you?"

"I'm Daisy," I said slowly. "And I'm definitely not the owner."

"I'm Mason." He tilted his head, frowning at me. "You're sure you're not Hanna?"

"Pretty sure."

"Then why are you in my rental?"

I pulled out my phone, waving the screenshot of my confirmation email like evidence in a court case. "I rented this cabin for the week. I have a reservation. I paid a deposit. This place is mine."

Mason set down his spatula and reached into his back pocket, producing a piece of paper that he unfolded. "That's funny," he said, his tone still friendly but now edged with uncertainty. "Because according to this, I also rented this cabin for the week. I spend my Christmas here almost every year."

I stared at the confirmation email. It was identical to mine except for the name and credit card information. Same dates. Same cabin. Same booking reference number that should have been unique.

"This is impossible," I muttered, scrolling through my phone to double-check my own reservation. I tugged at my hair tie, pulling it tighter until my scalp ached. "Booking systems don't just double-book. There are safeguards. Protocols."

"Apparently not foolproof ones," Mason said with a smile. "Look, I've been here since yesterday, but there's plenty of space. The cabin's got a big bed and a couch, and I'm a pretty quiet roommate. We could—"

"No." The word came out sharper than I'd intended. "No, we could not. I came here specifically to avoid people. All people. That was the entire point."

Mason's eyebrows rose, but his expression remained patient. "I can see that. But unless one of us wants to drive back down the mountain in this weather—" He gestured toward the window, where snow was now falling in thick, heavy flakes. "—we might not have much choice."

I looked outside at the snow that was getting heavier by the minute. The kind of snow that turned mountain roads into death traps. The kind that triggered very specific, very unwelcome memories of losing control, of the world spinning beyond my ability to stop it.

My chest tightened, and I forced myself to take a slow breath through my nose. This was fine. This was manageable. I just needed to think logically about the situation and find a solution that didn't involve sharing space with a stranger who seemed entirely too comfortable with the very inconvenient circumstances.

And who smelled like cedar and coffee and made my pulse skip in ways that had nothing to do with panic. Nothing at all.

"There has to be another option," I said, already pulling up the rental company's website on my phone. Or rather, I *tried* to pull up the rental company's website. No signal. In the mix-up, I'd already forgotten about the other terrifying factor in this situation. Isolation. Complete and utter isolation.

"I tried calling them this morning about a question about the fireplace," Mason said as if he'd read my mind. "No luck. We're pretty cut off up here. Every once in a while a signal will go through, but it's not often."

I switched my attention from him, to the snow outside, then to my bags sitting in the entryway of what was supposed to be my forced perfect, solitary retreat. The bacon was starting to smell incredible, and despite everything, my traitorous stomach chose that moment to growl loudly.

Mason's grin returned, softer this time. "Look, I know this isn't what either of us planned. But I make really good coffee, I clean up after myself, and I promise I'm much better company than hypothermia."

"Are you always this optimistic about disasters?"

"I prefer to think of this as an unexpected adventure." He shrugged. "Plus, I'm always open to new friends, especially around the holidays."

I looked at him again. Really looked this time. He had laugh lines around his eyes and flour on his shirt, and despite my general state of panic, there was something oddly reassuring about his presence. Like he was the kind of person who would know what to do if the power went out or a bear wandered onto the porch. Not the kind of person who would stab me in the shower or suffocate me in my sleep. I hoped...

Still. Sharing a cabin with a complete stranger was not part of the plan. Especially not a complete stranger who made me notice things like the way his thermal shirt stretched across his chest when he moved.

"How many bedrooms did you say?" I asked reluctantly.

"One. It's upstairs, but I'll move my stuff and take the couch. That way—"

"No. The couch is fine."

"Uh." He gave me a once over and shook his head. "Absolutely not. I won't have a lady sleeping on the couch. Not when there's a perfectly good bed." He held up a large hand when I opened my mouth to argue. "Nope. Me couch. You bed."

"But you were here first." I crossed my arms, even as my stomach did that flippy thing. He was offering to be a gentleman, and yet my stubborn mouth wouldn't shut up. I didn't want the couch. I wanted a bed.

"Doesn't matter. Until we get this figured out, you take the bed. I'll move my things out of there once we're done eating." He nodded his head as if the decision were final, and then gestured towards the spread of food on the counter.

"So what exactly is the plan then? What are you suggesting?" I asked.

"I'm suggesting we make the best of it," Mason said, his smile widening. "Two reasonable adults, one cozy cabin, enough food for a small army. We can coexist for a few days until the roads clear and we can sort this out properly."

"Make the best of it," I repeated slowly, as if the words might make more sense if I said them out loud. They didn't. "You want me to share a cabin with a complete stranger for an entire week."

"Well, when you put it like that, it sounds terrible," he said, taking another sip of his coffee. "But look at it this way; we're both here because we needed to get away from something. We can stay out of each other's way, enjoy some peace and quiet, and pretend this was all part of some cosmic plan."

As if to prove his point, the wind chose that moment to rattle the windows, and I caught a glimpse of the snow swirling past in thick, almost horizontal sheets.

"This is not how my vacation was supposed to start," I muttered.

"Most good adventures don't start the way you expect them to."

I wanted to argue, to insist that I didn't want an adventure, that I was forced into this. That all I wanted was a predictable, solitary week of decompression. But the truth was that driving back down that mountain in this weather would be suicide. And not the metaphorical kind.

"Fine," I said, the word coming out like I was agreeing to voluntary surgery. "But we need ground rules."

"Ground rules?" Mason's eyebrows went up, but he didn't look surprised.

"Schedules," I said, already pulling out my phone to open my notes app. "Kitchen usage, bathroom time, common areas. We need to coordinate so we're not tripping over each other."

"Or," Mason said, drawing the word out, "we could just be considerate adults and ask before we do anything that might interfere with each other."

I stared open mouthed at him like he'd suggested we set the cabin on fire. "That's not a system."

"No," he agreed. "It's trust."

Trust. Another one of those words that shouldn't exist in the context of strangers sharing confined spaces. Trust was what got you hurt. Trust was what led to cars running red lights and lives getting turned upside down in the space of a heartbeat.

But looking at Mason, with his easy smile and his offer to cook breakfast for a stranger, I wondered if maybe I could manage it for a week.

"Fine," I said, the word coming out strangled. "We'll... figure it out as we go."

Mason's smile could have powered the cabin for a month.

"See?" he said. "You're already getting the hang of this vacation thing."

I wasn't sure about that. But as he handed me a plate of the most perfect pancakes I'd ever seen, I had to admit that maybe this week wasn't going to kill me after all.

"By the way," Mason said as I took my first bite, "I should probably mention, I'm a photographer. Wildlife, mostly. I'll probably be out with my camera quite a bit, so you'll have plenty of solitude."

"What kind of wildlife?"

"Whatever's out there. Though right now I'm hoping for some good winter bird shots. Maybe catch some of the ice formations up the creek if the weather cooperates." His expression grew more serious. "Actually, I should tell you, this assignment is pretty important for me.

I'm trying to build a portfolio strong enough for National Geographic. It's kind of a make-or-break opportunity."

"National Geographic," I repeated. "That's... big."

"Biggest break I could ask for. If I can nail this winter series, it could change everything." Mason's expression turned self-deprecating. "No pressure or anything. Just my entire career hanging in the balance."

"Well," I said, cutting another bite of pancake, "I guess we're both here for important reasons then."

"Guess so. What's yours?"

"Proving to my boss that I won't have a nervous breakdown if I stop working for five minutes."

Mason's laugh was warm and genuine. "Think you'll manage it?"

"Ask me in a week."

As I ate his perfect pancakes and watched him move around the kitchen with easy competence, I couldn't help but notice the small details that suggested he was more prepared for mountain living than most people. A well-stocked first aid kit visible on the counter. Emergency candles and matches arranged neatly by the window. A weather radio sitting next to the coffee maker.

"You seem pretty well-equipped for someone who just got here yesterday," I observed.

Mason glanced at the items I was noticing and shrugged. "Boy Scout training never really leaves you. Plus, when you spend as much time in remote locations as I do, you learn to be prepared for anything. Power outages, sudden weather changes, equipment failures. It's all part of the job."

"You were a Boy Scout?"

"Eagle Scout, actually. My mom insisted." He grinned. "She said if I was going to spend my life wandering around in the wilderness, I better know how to take care of myself and anyone else who might need help."

The way he said it made me wonder what other skills he might have that could come in handy in an isolated mountain cabin. The thought was oddly comforting, though I wasn't quite ready to admit that to myself yet.

"I just hope you're not a morning person," I mumbled as I shoveled another bite of pancakes into my mouth.

# Make Sure To Check Out Maggie Ellis's First Christmas Novella

MAGGIE ELLIS

## The Christmas Cabin Mix-Up

A CUTE HOLIDAY NOVELLA

# Make Sure To Check Out All 3 Cute Fall Romcoms With The Thatcher Brothers!

# Acknowledgments

To my husband, who is my quiet supporter and the inspiration for Asher. To the love of my life, who makes me laugh and indulges me when I spend hours telling him about the voices in my head waiting for their stories to be told. You are my person and I love you.

Thank you to my incredible beta readers who made this book (and the first two) so much better with their helpful feedback, funny comments, and support: Rachel H., Becca L., and Jenn C.—you're wonderful and I love you.

And to my dog, who continues to be my writing buddy and lap warmer. You are the best pupper a dog mom could ask for.

Of course, the biggest thank you to you, sweet reader. May your coffee be perfect, your books entertaining, and your fall days lovely.

With love,

**Maggie**

*IF YOU ENJOYED THIS
SWEET FALL ROMCOM,
PLEASE CONSIDER
LEAVING A REVIEW.
IT HELPS OUT A TON!*

# About the Author

Maggie Ellis writes swoony, clean romantic comedies filled with awkward meet-cutes, heartfelt moments, and more than a few cups of coffee. When she's not dreaming up cute romances, she can usually be found baking something unnecessarily complicated, wandering through independent bookstores, or losing another sock to the dryer gremlins. She lives in a small town where everyone waves and the Wi-Fi is questionable, but the inspiration is endless.

www.ingramcontent.com/pod-product-compliance
Lightning Source LLC
Chambersburg PA
CBHW021111130626
46554CB00002B/643